"For old times' sake."

He whispered the words as his arms slipped around her on the dance floor.

As she stepped into his familiar embrace, his woodsy aftershave snaked around her, and he held her captive in his warmth and the seductive sway of his body.

Ian was an amazing lover, a good man, and she cared about him far more than was good for her.

Could they find a way to raise their baby?

She'd never thought that loving Ian and living in Brighton Valley for the rest of her life would be enough. But now she wondered how she could give him up.

"Come on," he whispered. "Let's go home."

Desire crackled between them all the way to the ranch, and even though Carly tried to ignore it, to tell Ian good-night, something stronger overrode her common sense.

She invited him in for coffee.

But once they entered the house, she didn't go to the kitchen. Instead, she turned to face the man who'd fathered her baby and touched her heart.

Every part of her brain told her she was about to make a mistake. A big mistake. But it was a mistake she couldn't live without.

* * *

BRIGHTON VALLEY COWBOYS: This Texas family is looking for love in all the right places!

P9-DJL-857

Dear Reader,

In Brighton Valley, the Rayburn heirs are still sorting through Granny's heirlooms, as well as recreating a relationship with each other. Unfortunately, Carly Rayburn is struggling with more than the family dynamics between her and her half brothers. She's also dealing with a growing attraction to her old lover.

All Carly has ever wanted is to stand out on her own and to be recognized as more than the girl whose divorced parents were too busy with their own lives to spend time with her. Yet her dream of a career in country music is thrown off course when she learns she's pregnant by a handsome cowboy who has no intention of picking up roots.

Ten years ago, Ian McAllister was known as "Mac," a guitarist and songwriter for a famous country singer. But he grew tired of it all and left Nashville behind for the life of a cowboy. At the Leaning R, he's found the perfect place to hide—until a beautiful singer who's determined to find the fame he left behind throws his plans out of whack.

If you like cowboys, babies and family secrets, you're going to enjoy reading Ian and Carly's story. And if you're eager to find a recipe for Granny's Texas Chocolate Cake, you'll find it posted on my website, JudyDuarte.com

Happy 2016—and happy reading!

Judy Duarte

PS: I love hearing from my readers. Contact me on facebook.com/JudyDuarteNovelist.

Having the Cowboy's Baby

Judy Duarte

HARLEQUIN® SPECIAL EDITION®

Recycling programs
for this product may
not exist in your area.

ISBN-13: 978-0-373-65932-6

Having the Cowboy's Baby

Printed in U.S.A.

Since 2002, *USA TODAY* bestselling author **Judy Duarte** has written over forty books for Harlequin Special Edition, earned two RITA® Award finals, won two Maggies and received a National Readers' Choice Award. When she's not cooped up in her writing cave, she enjoys traveling with her husband and spending quality time with her grandchildren. You can learn more about Judy and her books at her website, judyduarte.com, or at facebook.com/judyduartenovelist.

Books by Judy Duarte

Harlequin Special Edition

Brighton Valley Cowboys

The Boss, the Bride & the Baby

Return to Brighton Valley

The Soldier's Holiday Homecoming
The Bachelor's Brighton Valley Bride
The Daddy Secret

The Fortunes of Texas: Cowboy Country

A Royal Fortune

The Fortunes of Texas: Welcome to Horseback Hollow

A House Full of Fortunes!

The Fortunes of Texas: Southern Invasion

Marry Me, Mendoza

Byrds of a Feather

Tammy and the Doctor

Brighton Valley Babies

The Cowboy's Family Plan
The Rancher's Hired Fiancée
A Baby Under the Tree

The Fortunes of Texas: Whirlwind Romance

Mendoza's Miracle

Brighton Valley Medical Center

Race to the Altar
His, Hers and...Theirs?
Under the Mistletoe with John Doe

Visit the Author Profile page at Harlequin.com for more titles.

To my daughter, Christy Jeffries, who is everything I could ever wish for in a daughter and more.

Congratulations on your sales to Special Edition, the first of which—*A Marine for His Mom*—shares a January release date with my book! I'm looking forward to sharing more of the crazy and fabulous life of being a Harlequin author with you.

Chapter One

Carly Rayburn was back in town. Not that there'd been any big announcements, but news traveled fast in Brighton Valley. And even if it didn't, not much got past Ian McAllister.

She'd had a singing gig in San Antonio, but apparently that hadn't panned out for her, which was too bad. She had a dream to make it big in country music someday, a dream Ian no longer had. But he couldn't fault her for that.

Jason, her oldest brother, said she'd be staying on the Leaning R for a while, which wasn't a surprise. It seemed to Ian that she came home to the ranch whenever her life hit a snag. So that's what she would do, right after attending Jason's wedding in town.

As the foreman of the Leaning R, Ian had been

invited to the ceremony and reception, but he'd graciously declined and sent a gift instead. The only people attending were family and a few close friends, so Ian would have felt out of place—for more reasons than one. So he'd remained on the ranch.

Now, as darkness settled over Brighton Valley, he did what he often did in the evenings after dinner. He sat on the front porch of his small cabin and enjoyed the peaceful evening sounds, the scent of night-blooming jasmine and the vast expanse of stars in the Texas sky.

The Leaning R had been in Carly's family for years. It was run-down now, but it had great potential. It was also the perfect place for Ian to hide out, where people only knew him as a quiet cowboy who felt more comfortable around livestock than the bright lights of the big cities. And thanks to his granddaddy, who'd once owned a respectable spread near Dallas, that was true.

He glanced at the Australian shepherd puppy nestled in his lap. The sleepy pooch yawned, then stretched and squirmed.

"What's the matter, Cheyenne?" He stroked her black-and-white furry head. "Is your snooze over?"

When the pup gave a little yip, Ian set her down and watched as she padded around the wooden flooring, taking time to sniff at the potted geranium on the porch, her stub of a tail wagging. Then she waddled down the steps.

"Don't wander off too far," he told her. "It's dark out there, and you're still getting the lay of the land."

The pup glanced at him, as if she understood what he was saying, then trotted off.

Ian loved dogs. He'd grown up with several of them on his granddad's ranch, but after he'd moved out on his own, he hadn't been able to have one until now. Fortunately, his life was finally lining up the way he'd always hoped it would. Once the Leaning R went on the market, as Carly's brother said it would, Ian was prepared to buy it. As the trustee and executor of the Rayburn family estate, Jason was in charge now. The only thing holding him back from listing the property was getting Carly and their brother Braden to agree to the sale.

But Braden had his own spread about ten miles down the road, and Carly had no intention of being a rancher. When she'd left Brighton Valley the last time, she'd been hell-bent on making a name for herself. With her talent, there was no reason she wouldn't. There was always a price for fame, though, and Ian just hoped she was willing to pay it.

He reached for his guitar, which rested beside him near the cabin window, and settled it into his lap. As he strummed the new song he'd written, the chords filled the peaceful night. He might love ranching, but that didn't mean he'd given up music altogether. He just played for pleasure these days, in the evenings after a long workday. He'd learned the hard way that it beat the hell out of opening a bottle of whiskey to relax.

Now, as he sat outside singing the words to the tune he'd written about love gone wrong, he waited for Carly to return from the wedding she'd come home to attend, waited to see if anything had changed. To see if, by some strange twist of fate, she'd decided that she wanted something different out of life.

He'd only played a few bars when his cell phone rang. He set the guitar aside and answered on the third ring.

"Hey, Mac," the graveled smoker's voice said. "How's it going?"

It was Uncle Roy, one of the few people who called him Mac and who knew how to contact him. "Not bad. How's everything in Sarasota? How are Grandma and Granddad?"

"They're doing just fine. Mama's cholesterol is a bit high, but the doctor put her on some medication to lower it. Other than that, they're settling into retired life out here in Florida and making friends."

Ian was glad to hear it, although he'd been sorry when his grandparents had sold the family ranch. But his granddad had put in a long, successful life, first as a rodeo cowboy, then as a rancher. And Grandma had always wanted to live near the water. So Ian couldn't blame him for selling the place and moving closer to his sole remaining son—even if Ian felt more like his uncle's sibling than a nephew.

"Say," Roy said, "I called to let you know that it'll be their fiftieth wedding anniversary next month—on the fifteenth. So me and your aunt Helen are planning a party for them. We're going to try to keep it a surprise, although I'm not sure if we can pull it off. But it'd be great if you could come."

"I'll be there." Ian wasn't sure what he'd do about finding someone to look after the Leaning R for him, but there was no way he'd miss celebrating with the couple who'd raised him.

"Dad said you're thinking about buying that place where you've been working," Roy added.

"That's my plan."

"You made an offer yet?"

"Not yet." But Ian was ready to jump the minute the place was officially on the market.

"What's the holdup?"

"The ranch is held by a trust, and the trustees are three half siblings. They're not quite in agreement about selling. At least, they didn't used to be. I think it's finally coming together now."

"What *was* the holdup?"

"A couple of them wanted it to stay in the family, but no one was willing to move in and take over."

Uncle Roy seemed to chew on that for a while, then asked, "You sure it's a good deal?"

"Damned straight. The widow of the man who originally owned it took good care of it, but her grandson, the previous trustee, was some sort of big-shot, corporate-exec type who let it go to the dogs. It's a shame, too. You should have seen what it once was—and what it could become again with a little love and cash. I'm looking forward to having the right to invest in it the way Mrs. Rayburn would have if she were still alive."

"Well, Helen and I'll be praying for you. I hope it all works out. I know having your own place and running a spread has been a dream of yours for a long time."

And that dream had grown stronger these past three years. "Thanks, Uncle Roy."

"Never did understand why you wanted to give up the good life, though. Dad says you were always a rancher at heart and not a performer. And he knows you best. But damn, boy. You sure could play and sing."

Ian still could. It was the fame he'd never liked. He'd always been an introvert, and even though he hadn't been the lead singer in the group, the gigs had gotten harder and harder to handle without a couple of shots of tequila to get him through the night.

So when the lights had grown too bright, the crowds too big and his fear of following in his alcoholic father's stumbling boot steps too real, he'd left the groupies and Nashville behind for the quiet life of a cowboy.

"Listen, I gotta go," Roy said.

"Give everyone my love. I know it's an hour later there and Granddad turns in early, so I'll call them in the morning."

"Don't forget—that party's a secret," Roy added.

"I won't."

When the line disconnected, Ian scanned the yard for Cheyenne, only to find her sniffing around near the faucet in the middle of the yard. Then he began strumming his guitar again.

Not everyone understood why he'd given up the life he'd once led, but Ian was happy here on the Leaning R. Only trouble was, Carly had swept into his life and turned it upside down for a while.

And now she was back.

Carly Rayburn gripped the wheel of her red Toyota Tacoma, the radio filling the cab with the latest country-western hit. She was still dressed in the pale green dress she'd worn as the maid of honor at her half brother's wedding, although she'd slipped on a denim jacket to ward off the evening chill and traded her high heels for her favorite pair of cowboy boots.

Under normal circumstances, she usually came up with an excuse for why she couldn't attend weddings. For one reason, she found it difficult to feign happiness for the bride and groom because she was skeptical of the whole "until death do us part" philosophy.

But then, why wouldn't she be? Her father had a daughter and two sons by three different women. Then, after her parents' divorce, her mom had gone on to date a series of men, all celebrities who'd moved in and out of Carly's life as if it were a revolving door. So was it any wonder she thought "true love" was a myth and only something to sing about?

Today, however, when she stood at the altar and watched her oldest brother, Jason, vow to love, honor and cherish Juliana Bailey for the rest of their lives, she had to admit to not only being surprised by the rush of sentiment, but also feeling hopeful for the newlyweds, too. And that was a first.

Now, as she steered her pickup toward the Leaning R Ranch, she found herself happy for Jason and Juliana yet pondering her own future, which was now up in the air. Five weeks ago, she'd thought she'd finally gotten her start with a singing gig at a nightclub in San Antonio, but a stomach bug had ended that, leaving her between jobs again.

For the most part, she felt a lot better now. But every

time she thought the virus was a thing of the past, it flared up again. Like today, at her brother's reception. She was going to have a glass of champagne, but before she could even take a sip, a whiff of the popping bubbles set off her nausea. Yet now she was fine again.

When she'd first caught the flu or whatever it was, she'd gotten sick right before showtime in San Antonio. Her friend, Heather, had suggested that it might be stage fright, but there was no way that was the case. Carly had been performing ever since she could stand in front of her bedroom mirror and grip the mic on her child's karaoke machine.

She figured she was just tired and run-down. So, with a little R & R on her family's ranch, she'd kick this thing in no time at all and line up another gig before you could sing "Back in the Saddle Again."

When she got within a few miles of the ranch, her thoughts drifted to Ian, the handsome cowboy who was content living on the Leaning R and who had no intention of picking up stakes. The two of them had become intimately involved the last time she came home, and as nice as it had been, as heated, as *magical*, Carly didn't dare let it start up again.

So for that reason, she'd dragged her feet at the wedding reception, which was held at Maestro's, the new Italian restaurant on Main Street. It was a nice venue for a small but elegant celebration—probably too nice and upscale for Brighton Valley, though. Still, while everyone had raved about the food, she thought the chef had been way too heavy-handed with the garlic and basil. Just one sniff had caused her to push her plate aside. But then, she'd had a late lunch and hadn't been all that hungry anyway.

Once the newlyweds had taken off in a limousine bound for Houston, Carly had climbed into her pickup and left town. According to her plan, she would arrive at the Leaning R after dark, when it would be less likely for anyone—namely Ian—to see her. She just hoped she could slip unnoticed into the house and remain there until she figured out a plan B.

Yet, as luck would have it, when she pulled into the graveled drive at the Leaning R, Ian's lights blazed bright. And to make matters worse, he was sitting on the front porch of his cabin.

That meant she would have to face the one man in Brighton Valley who unwittingly had the power to thwart most any plan she might come up with—if she let him. But there was no chance of that. Maybe if she'd been like the other girls who grew up around here, content to settle for the country life on a homestead with some cowboy and their two-point-four kids, she'd be champing at the bit to let the sexy foreman make an honest woman of her. But Carly had never been like the other girls—her family life had been too dysfunctional—and she was even less like them now. She had big dreams to go on world tours, while Ian was content to stay in Brighton Valley.

Well, there was no avoiding him now. She got out of the truck and made her way toward his small cabin.

"Hey," she said. "How's it going?"

"All right." He set his guitar aside. "How was the wedding?"

"Small, but nice. That is, if you're into that sort of thing."

"And you're not." It was a statement, not a question. Ian was well aware of how Carly felt about love and forever-after, so she let it go with a half shrug. His easygoing and nonjudgmental attitude was the main reason she'd even allowed herself to have a brief fling with him four or five months back. Well, that and the way he looked in those faded jeans.

He'd taken off his hat, revealing thick, brown hair in need of a comb. Or a woman's touch.

She'd always found his green eyes intriguing—the way they lit up in mirth, the intensity in them during the heat of lovemaking.

His gaze raked over her as if he was hoping to pick up where they'd left off, and her heart rate stumbled before catching on to the proper beat again. But then, the guitar wasn't the only thing Ian was skilled at strumming.

If truth be told, there'd been a fleeting moment at the wedding when her own resolve had waffled. She'd seen her stuffy brother's eyes light up when his pretty bride walked down the aisle, and it had had touched her heart. She truly hoped that Jason and Juliana defied the odds and lived happily ever after. But she just couldn't quite see herself dressed in white lace and making lifelong promises to someone. After all, she'd never known anyone who'd actually met "the one" and managed to make a commitment that had lasted longer than a year or two.

She glanced at Ian, saw his legs stretched out while

seated in that patio chair, all long and lean, muscle and sinew. She did love a handsome cowboy, though. And Ian certainly fit the image to a tee. He also knew how to treat a lady—in all the ways that mattered.

Again, she shook it off. They'd ended things on a good note, both of them agreeing that their sexual fling—no matter how good it had been—would only end awkwardly if they let it go on any further. It had been a mutual agreement that she had every intention of sticking to.

"That's an interesting bridesmaid getup," he said as his gaze swept down to her boots and back up again.

"A bridesmaid *getup*?" That was a cowboy for you. "The wedding was so sudden that I didn't have time to shop. So I wore a dress I've had for a while." She glanced at her skirt, then twirled slightly to the right. "What's wrong with it?"

"Not a thing." His lips quirked into a crooked grin. "I was talking about the denim jacket and the boots. Juliana and Jason seem to be more traditional."

She smiled. "Well, that's true. I kicked off my heels the first chance I got. And since it's a bit chilly out tonight and this dress is sleeveless, I grabbed the only jacket I had handy."

"Either way, you make a good-looking bridesmaid, Carly."

Before she could change the subject to one that was much safer than brides or commitments of any kind, she noticed a bush at the side of the cabin shake and tremble.

Had that pesky raccoon come back again? If so,

it was certainly getting brave. But instead of Rocky, the nickname she and Ian had for the little rascal that knocked over the trash cans, a darling little black-and-white puppy trotted out from the bush.

"Oh my gosh," Carly said. "How cute is he?"

"It's a she. And her name is Cheyenne."

As Carly bent to pick up the pup, she must have moved too quickly, because a wave of dizziness struck. For a moment, everything around her seemed to spin. She wasn't going to faint, was she?

She paused a moment and blinked. Her head cleared, thank goodness. Then she pulled the hem of her dress out of the way, slowly got on her knees and reached out her hands. The pup came right over to her, but she held still for a while longer, making sure the world wouldn't start spinning again.

"Aren't you a sweetheart?" she said to the puppy. Then she glanced at Ian, who had a boyish grin splashed across his face. "Where'd you get her?"

"Paco, the owner of the feed store, had a litter of Australian shepherds for sale, so I bought her. It's something I've been planning to do for a while. A spread like this needs a good cattle dog."

Carly pulled the pup into her arms and stood. "But what if the new owners don't want you to stay on?"

He shrugged. "I'm not worried."

Ian didn't get too concerned about much. In fact, he always seemed to go with the flow, which was a plus in the casual relationship department, but another reason they'd never make a good match in the long run. He didn't have the same ambition she did.

For as long as Carly could remember, all she'd wanted was to stand out on her own and be recognized as more than a pretty little girl whose divorced parents, a wealthy businessman and a glamorous country-western singer, were both too busy to spend quality time with her. And she'd found the best place to do that was on the stage.

"That puppy is going to get your pretty dress all dirty," Ian said.

"I don't mind." She tossed him a smile as Cheyenne licked her nose. "I've always wanted a dog, but I never stay in one place long enough to have one."

"I'll share Cheyenne with you when you come home."

As nice as the offer was, it wouldn't work. "Jason plans to sell the ranch, remember?"

"Yep. I sure do."

"So I won't have a place to run home to anymore. At least, it won't be here. And like I said, you don't know for sure that the new owner will want you to stay on. I mean, I hope they do."

"Like I said…" His eyes sparkled, and a grin tickled his lips. "I'm not worried."

"Yes, but you have to be responsible for a puppy now."

"Having something to look after will do me good."

She thought about some of the homeless people she'd seen on the city streets, pushing a grocery cart laden with their belongings, a tethered dog trotting along beside them. Not that she had any reason to think Ian would ever find himself homeless. He'd built a good reputation with the other ranchers in town. He was also a hard worker and would undoubtedly find a job somewhere. But he seemed to be as carefree as a tumble-weed, especially when it came to making plans, which was yet another reason they'd never make a go of it. Their basic personalities were just too different.

"You're going to find that the ranch house is nearly all packed," Ian said. "Juliana had most everything boxed up by the time she left. So it might not be too comfortable sleeping in there. But you're welcome to stay with me, if you want."

Memories of the nights she'd spent in his bed swept over her, warming her blood and setting a flutter in her tummy. But that wouldn't do either of them any good. Well, maybe it would for as long as it lasted, but she couldn't afford to get too invested in him—or anyone—at this stage in her career.

"As tempting as that might be," she said, "I'd better pass. Besides, Juliana told me the kitchen is still in order. And the guest bed has fresh sheets. So I'll be okay."

"Suit yourself."

Their gazes locked for a moment, as a lover's moon shone brightly overhead. And while Ian didn't say another word, she felt compelled to continue arguing her case.

"We already discussed this," she said.

His smile dimpled his cheeks in a way that could tempt a good girl to rebel. "I didn't say anything about sleeping with me, although I won't turn you down if you insist."

She clicked her tongue and returned his smile.

"You're incorrigible, Ian McAllister. You're going to be the death of me."

"No, I'm not. You said it yourself, a relationship between us would crash and burn. And I agreed."

He had, and it was true. But that didn't lessen her attraction to him, which seemed to be just as strong as it ever had been. She'd just have to ratchet up her willpower and avoid him whenever possible.

So she walked up to the porch and placed Cheyenne next to his chair. As she did so, she caught a whiff of soap and leather, musk and cowboy. Dang, downplaying their chemistry wasn't going to be easy.

He reached for her hand, and as he did, his thumb grazed her wrist. Her heart quickened.

"It's good to have you back, Carly. I missed your company."

She'd missed him, too. The horseback rides, the sing-alongs on his porch, the lovemaking in his cabin, the mornings waking up in his arms... But she tugged her hand from his grip. She didn't have to pull very hard. She was free from his touch before she knew it.

"Well, I'd better turn in," she said. "It's been a long day."

"Good night."

No argument? Not that she wanted one. But she was used to men coming on to her.

So why wasn't she relieved that he'd taken no for an answer so easily?

Because life got complicated when hormones got in the way of good judgment, that's why.

"Sleep tight," she said as she turned and started for the house.

The chords of his guitar rang out in the night as he played a lively melody with a two-step beat, a tune she didn't recognize, a song she'd never heard. She turned, crossed her arms and shifted her weight to one hip. When she did, he stopped playing.

"That's nice," she said. "Is it something you wrote?"

"Yep. You like it?"

"I really do. You have a lot of talent, Ian. You ought to do something with it."

"I just did. And you heard it."

"That's not what I meant. You should let me—or somebody—record this song. Maybe it could be a hit."

"You have a beautiful voice, Carly. But I'm not interested in recording this song. It's something I wrote for my grandparents. It's going to be my gift to them."

"That's great, and I'll bet they'll love it. But what if you could do even more with it? Wouldn't that be an awesome tribute to them?"

"I'd like them to be the first to hear it performed at their wedding anniversary."

"But maybe afterward—"

"Sorry. My mind's made up."

So it was. And that should serve as a good reminder that Ian wasn't a go-getter like she was. Sure, he could put in the effort when it came to working the ranch, but he had no other goals besides living as simply as possible. Plus, she'd learned that, as carefree as Ian McAllister could be, he was as stubborn as Granny Rayburn's old milk cow when he *did* make a decision.

She nodded, then turned to go. As she made her way to the house, the melody followed her, and so did Ian's soulful voice as it sang of two lonely hearts finding each other one moonlit night, of them falling crazy in love and of the lifetime vow they'd made, one that would last forever and a day.

She would have liked to have met the couple that had inspired him to write such a beautiful song. If she had known them, maybe she would look forward to settling down herself one day. But not for a long time—and certainly not with Ian.

Chapter Two

When Carly entered the front door of the ranch house, unexpected grief struck her like a wallop to the chest.

The inside walls were lined with boxes stacked two and three high, each one carefully labeled with what was inside. Carly had known that her new sister-in-law had first inventoried and then packed up Granny's belongings, but that still hadn't prepared her for the heartbreaking sight.

Seeing a lifetime of memories all boxed up, especially the plaques, pictures and knickknacks that made the ranch a home, reminded her that Granny was gone and the Leaning R would soon belong to someone else. And for the first time in Carly's life, coming home wasn't the least bit comforting.

As she wandered through the empty house like a

lost child, the ache in her chest grew as hard and cold as dry ice.

Needing comfort—or a sense of place—she hurried to the kitchen, where she and Granny had spent a lot of time together. She nearly cried with joy at the familiar surroundings. It was the only room that still bore Granny's touch, the only place that still offered a safe haven from the disappointment of the outside world.

She studied the faded blue wallpaper, with its straw baskets holding wildflowers. The colors, now yellowed with age, had once brightened the kitchen where Carly had often joined Granny before mealtimes and begged to help her cook and bake.

The elderly woman had been more of a mother to Carly than the one who'd given birth to her and then left her in the care of nannies for most of her childhood. Of course, Raelynn Fallon would say that wasn't true. And no one argued with Raelynn, least of all her daughter, who'd been asked to refer to her by her first name because *Mama* made her sound so old and matronly.

Was it any wonder their mother-daughter relationship hadn't been all that warm and loving?

Thank God for Granny, who'd been the only parental role model Carly had ever had. For that reason, she'd grieved more for her great-grandma's passing last year than she had when word came of her father's fatal car accident in Mexico four months ago.

Carly glanced at the cat-shaped clock on wall, its drooping black tail swinging back and forth with each tick-tock.

Life went on, she supposed. But now she was at a loss. There'd been plenty to do on her last trip home, but that was no longer the case. Jason had hired Juliana to inventory and pack Granny's belongings before he'd fallen in love with the woman and married her. And while Carly was tempted to unpack the boxes and return everything to where it belonged, she couldn't very well do that.

So what was she going to do with her time, especially since she was trying to avoid Ian?

Her gaze landed on the countertop, where she spotted Granny's old recipe box. She reached for the familiar, white metal container, with the scene of a mountain meadow hand painted on the outside. She lifted the lid and studied the yellowed tabs, bent from use.

Appetizers, beverages, breads, cakes...

She thumbed through the cookie recipes, which had always been her favorites. Granny had made little handwritten notes on the back of most of them. What a treat to be able to read her great-grandmother's thoughts tonight, especially when she knew sleep wouldn't come easy.

After rummaging through the pantry for a box of herbal tea, Carly filled the teapot with water, then put it on the stove to heat. Next, she took a seat at the antique oak table to begin reading through Granny's recipes as well as the notes on the backs of them.

She'd no more than pulled out the stack of cards listed under cookies when her cell phone rang. She glanced at the display. It was Heather, who was still performing in the show in San Antonio, the one Carly had once starred in and then had to quit.

"Hey," Carly said. "What's up?"

"I called to check on you. How are you feeling?"

"A lot better, although I've been pretty tired lately. I think that's from burning the candle at both ends— and that bug I had really wore me down."

"You probably ought to talk to a doctor."

"I plan to get some sleep while I'm on the ranch. I never rest as well as I do out here. If that doesn't work, I'll make an appointment to see mine."

"But how are you feeling otherwise? I mean, starring in that show was really important to you. And the director wasn't happy when you had to quit. Wasn't he the one who told you he'd put in a good word for you with his buddy in Nashville?"

"Yes, he was. So I doubt that he'll do that now. But I've been disappointed before." By people, by life events. Fortunately, Carly had learned to shake it off and to pivot in a new direction, if she needed to. "Don't worry. I'll find another gig soon."

"Good. You really need to get your career jumpstarted before you get to feeling maternal and lay that dream aside for a husband who doesn't appreciate you and a slew of whining kids."

Heather, who'd grown up as the oldest in a family of seven, had spent more time babysitting her younger siblings than being a child herself. So it wasn't any wonder she felt that way.

If truth be told, Carly had once dreamed of having a family of her own someday, with two kids, a dog and a house in the suburbs. She'd also told herself she'd find a husband who would be willing to co-parent and who'd promise not to work or be absent on holidays. But two years ago, her gynecologist had nipped that wishful thinking in the bud when she'd told Carly that due to a hormonal imbalance and a sketchy menstrual cycle she probably wouldn't ever be able to conceive.

But true to form, Carly had shaken off that girlish dream, instead focusing on her career. Besides, she'd told herself, with the lack of parenting she'd experienced, what kind of mother would she make anyway?

"Don't worry about me falling in love and giving up my singing career, Heather. I'll make it happen."

"I'm glad to hear it. And I love your can-do attitude." Her friend blew out a sigh. "But please give me a call after you talk to the doctor. I've been worried about you."

Now that Granny was gone, there weren't too many people who actually worried about Carly. She suspected Braden did, and Jason. The two of them had become a lot closer lately, especially since love and romance had softened her oldest brother.

"Thanks, Heather. If it turns out that I have to make an appointment, I'll let you know."

When she disconnected the call, Carly glanced down at the recipe cards in her hand. She flipped through them until she spotted one of her favorites.

Sugar cookies. What fun Carly used to have rolling out the dough and cutting them into shapes, especially at Christmas. Then she and Granny would frost them. She turned over the card. In blue ink, Granny had written:

Carly's favorite. The holidays aren't the same without these cookies. That precious child's eyes light up in pure joy. Warms my heart so.

Then, in pencil, she'd added: "It was a sad day when she grew too old to bake with me anymore."

Carly remembered Granny's last Christmas. She'd called and invited her to come over and bake cookies. "Just for old times' sake," Granny had added.

But Carly had been too busy. It hadn't been the first time she'd declined to visit Granny or to spend time in this old kitchen, but it had certainly been the last.

Was that the day Granny had penciled the note?

Guilt welled up in Carly's chest until it clogged her throat and brought tears to her eyes.

"Granny," she said aloud, "I'm going to bake a batch of sugar cookies for old times' sake. And before your kitchen is packed away."

Carly set the card aside and pulled out another. Brownies. No one made them like Granny. And this particular recipe had a fudge frosting that was to die for. On the back, Granny had written, "Men and boys can't say no to these! They make good peace offerings. And good bribes, too!"

The teapot on the stove whistled. After setting aside a stack of recipes she intended to bake, including Granny's Texas chocolate cake, Carly poured a cup of hot water into a cup, then tore open a packet of chamomile tea and let it steep.

With nothing on her agenda for this trip home—and most of the packing already done—she reached into the kitchen desk drawer, pulled out a sheet of paper and a pen. Then she began a long grocery list.

She had no idea what she was going to do with everything she intended to bake, but it was going to do her heart good. And right now, her heart needed all the good it could get.

As the summer sun climbed high in the Texas sky, Ian came out of the barn with Cheyenne tagging behind him. Carly had taken off a couple of hours ago, but he'd been in the south pasture at the time and had only watched her pickup driving down the county road.

He had no right to know where she was going, he supposed, but that didn't make him any less curious.

Still, as he headed for the corral, where Jesse Ramirez, one of the teenage boys Jason had hired, was painting the rails, Carly drove up. At least she hadn't taken one look at the packed-up house last night and blasted out of town at first light. Apparently, she planned to stick around for a while.

When she waved at him, his pulse spiked. But then why wouldn't it? Carly Rayburn was every cowboy's dream—a five-foot-two-inch blonde, blue-eyed beauty with a soft Southern twang and a body built for snug denim and white lace.

She was dressed to kill today in boots, black jeans and a blue frilly blouse. With her blond curls tumbling down her shoulders, she looked as though she was ready for one of the rides they used to take together, and he was half tempted to call it a day and suggest they do just that. But Carly had hitched her wagon to a different star and sought the fame and glory Ian had been happy to leave behind.

Of course, she had no idea who Ian had once been or why he'd given it all up. It was a secret he meant to keep now that he was living in small-town obscurity and going by his given name.

As she climbed from the truck and closed the driver's door, she said, "I don't suppose you'd want to help me carry some of this stuff into the house."

"Sure. What have you got there?"

"Groceries."

He glanced at the bags and boxes that filled the entire bed of her truck, then blew out a whistle. "What is all this? Flour, sugar, cocoa...? You planning to open a bakery?"

She laughed with that soft lilt that stirred his blood and lent a unique sound to her singing voice. "Maybe I should. I found Granny's recipe box last night. She made notes on the back of the cards. And since I couldn't sleep, I spent a long time reading over them and reminiscing. So I started making a grocery list, and... Well, it looks like I'm going to do some baking. I'll just have to find someone to give it to, or I'll end up looking like a Butterball turkey."

"Hey, don't forget where I live. I haven't had home-made goodies in ages. I favor chocolate, but I'm not fussy. If it's sweet, I'll give it a try."

She blessed him with a pretty smile. "I'll keep that in mind."

As they carried the groceries into the kitchen, she said, "Guess who I ran into at the market? Earl Tellis, the owner of the Stagecoach Inn."

"He was shopping?" Ian laughed. "I didn't figure him for being all that domestic."

"Neither did I, especially during daylight hours. But his wife had her appendix removed a couple of days ago, so he's helping out around the house."

Ian didn't respond. He sometimes drove out to the honky-tonk on weekend evenings, but for the most part, he didn't like crowds, especially as the night wore on and some folks tended to drink to excess and get rowdy. He'd certainly seen his share of it in the past. And he'd done his share of whooping it up, too. But he was pretty much a teetotaler now. He wanted to prove that he could say no and knew when to quit—unlike his old man.

"Earl asked if I'd come out and perform on Saturday night," Carly added.

"Good for you."

"Yeah, well, it's not the big time by any means, but it's a place to perform while I'm here." She bit down on her bottom lip.

Uh-oh. Ian had an idea where her thoughts were going.

"Earl asked if I had a band," she added. "I told him no, but that I might be able to find a guitarist."

"Who'd you have in mind?" He knew the answer, though, and his gut clenched.

"You, of course."

Ian shook his head. "I told you I'm not a performer."

"You don't know that yet—not if you don't try it first. Come on. Help me out this once. Without you, Earl's not going to want me." She bit down on her lip again, then blinked at him with those little ol' cocker spaniel eyes.

"Don't look at me like that."

Her lips parted, and her eyes grew wide. "Like what?"

He folded his arms across his chest. "I'm not your daddy who used to give in to that little sad face."

She slapped her hands on her denim clad hips and went from cocker spaniel to junkyard dog in nothing flat. "I'm not doing any such thing! And I never tried to work my dad like that."

Ian arched a brow in objection. "Come on, Carly. I saw you do it."

"When?"

"That first day you met me. When your dad stopped by and found out that the old foreman had retired and Granny chose me to replace him."

"My dad hadn't been happy to learn that Reuben Montoya had gone back to Mexico. And I was afraid he would do something…stupid."

"Like what?"

"Chase after him, I guess. Or fire you before we had a chance to see if you could handle Reuben's job." She gave a little shrug. "I was only trying to change the subject and give him something else to think about. But I didn't 'work' him the way you're implying."

"That wasn't the only time. And you were good at it, too. But it won't work on me."

"That's not fair, Ian. You make it sound like I'm a big flirt or a spoiled brat. And I'm neither."

Not by nature, he supposed. But when you grew up with an ultrarich father who thought throwing money at his kids was the same as saying I love you, it was probably hard not to try to get your way on occasion.

"I'm not trying to offend you or stir you up. And I don't want to thwart your chance at performing locally, but I'm not interested in playing guitar down at the Stagecoach Inn."

"Do you get nervous playing for a crowd?"

"Nope." Stage fright had never been an issue. "I just don't want to." That was the same reason he'd given Felicia Jamison, of country music fame, when he'd told her he was quitting the band. And she hadn't taken it any easier then than Carly was now. But he didn't figure he owed either of them any further explanation, although he probably should have given Felicia an earful.

Ten years ago, Felicia had been an up-and-coming singer when she'd hired Ian to be her lead guitarist. And the fit had been magical. Felicia could really rock the house with her voice, but it was Ian's songwriting that had helped her soar in popularity.

Most of her fans might not have heard of Mac McAllister, but he'd still earned a name for himself within the country music industry.

So far, no one in Brighton Valley knew who he was. Felicia had the face people would recognize. Ian had only been a member of her band, but if he put himself out in the limelight again, the greater chance he had of someone recognizing him and word of where he was getting out. And he'd been dead serious when he'd told Felicia that he was retiring.

"Then I guess you can't blame me if I try to change your mind," Carly said.

Ian wasn't sure how she intended to go about that, but the truth of the matter was, he still found Carly as sexy as hell. And while she'd made it clear that she didn't want their fling to start up all over again, he wasn't so sure he felt the same way.

Carly had never been one to take no for an answer— especially since she hadn't been entirely honest with Ian. Not only had Earl Tellis asked her to perform on Saturday night, but she'd already made the commitment—for both her *and* a guitarist.

And since Ian could be rather stubborn, she had her work cut out for her. She also had a batch of chewy, chocolaty brownies with fudge frosting that were sure to impress the handsome cowboy. After all, hadn't Granny said they made good bribes?

And that was exactly what Carly hoped to use them for this evening—a bribe to soften up Ian. So after dinner she put on a pretty yellow dress and slipped on her denim jacket and a pair of boots. Then she spent a little extra time on her makeup and hair before carrying a platter of brownies to his cabin.

Just like the night before, when she returned from the wedding, she found him sitting on his front porch, strumming his guitar. Only this time, he was playing a different tune, one that had a haunting melody, and singing the heart-stirring lyrics.

Not surprising, she thought it was just as memorable, just as good, as the one he'd written for his grandparents.

He stopped playing when she approached and cast her a heart-strumming smile instead.

"Was that another new song?" she asked, assuming it was and adjusting the platter in her arms.

"Yep."

Ian didn't realize how talented he was. Not only could he play and sing, but he had a way with lyrics, too. Most musicians would give up their birthrights to be able to write songs the way he could.

He set his guitar aside, next to where Cheyenne lay snoozing. "What do you have there? Did you bring dessert?"

Whoever said that the way to a man's heart was through his stomach must have been spot-on. She just hoped Granny's brownies were as persuasive as the note on the recipe suggested they were.

Carly stepped up on the porch and lifted the foil covering from the platter. "This is my first attempt to make Granny's blue-ribbon brownies. Tell me what you think."

Ian reached for one of the frosted squares and took a bite. As he chewed, his eyes closed and his expression morphed into one of such pleasure that she didn't need a verbal response. But when she got one, it was just what she'd expected.

"These are awesome, Carly. I had no idea you could bake like this."

She hoped he didn't get any ideas about her changing careers, because there was no way that would ever happen. "Thanks, but it was just a matter of following the directions on the recipe card. Granny was the baker in the family."

"That's for sure. A couple of days after I started working here, your great-grandmother asked me to have dinner with her." He burst into a broad grin, his eyes glimmering. "Fried chicken, mashed potatoes and gravy, fresh green beans. I'll never forget that meal—or any of the others that followed. I would have done anything Granny asked me to do just to get another invitation to sit at her table."

That's the magic Carly hoped the brownies would work for her. She offered Ian a warm smile. "Granny loved cooking and baking for people."

"She sure did. I really lucked out when I landed a job on the Leaning R. And not because I needed the work. I'd been homesick, so we kind of filled a need for each other."

Guilt swirled up inside again, twisting Carly's tummy into a knot. "I guess she was lonely after my brothers and I grew up and didn't need her to look after us anymore."

"She understood that kids should have a life of their own. But it was your father who seemed to abandon her. He got so caught up in his life and his business that she often felt neglected and forgotten."

"I know. Granny said as much to me. His parents

died in a small plane crash when he was a kid, and Granny raised him until his maternal grandfather insisted he attend college in California. That side of the family was very rich, and he was smitten by the glitz and glamour."

"Granny didn't hold that against him," Ian said. "But she still thought he should have called to check on her or stopped in to visit more often than he did."

Carly knew how the older woman felt. Heck, they all did. Charles Rayburn had been very generous with his money, but not with his time. And both of her brothers would agree.

"I hope I didn't let Granny down," she said.

"She never mentioned anything to me about you kids disappointing her."

Carly studied the handsome cowboy who seemed to have become her great-grandma's confidant at the end. "The two of you must have become pretty tight."

He gave a shrug. "I grew up with my grandparents, too. When I got tired of roaming and doing my own thing, I wanted to move back home. But by that time, Granddad had already retired, sold the ranch and moved to Florida to live near my uncle and his family. So I had to find another place to fall back on. That's when I met Granny. Three years ago. I was passing through Brighton Valley and stopped to have breakfast at Caroline's Diner. Granny needed an extra hand, and I wanted a job. Things ended up working out well for both of us."

"I guess it did. But there's something I've always wondered and never asked. Why did you stay on, especially now that things are so up in the air? It would seem to me that you'd look for work on a ranch that's more stable—and more successful."

Ian studied the pretty blonde, her curls tumbling along her shoulders, her blue eyes bright, the lashes thick and lush without the need for mascara.

She brushed the strand of hair from her eyes. "Was the question so difficult that you have to think about your answer? Most foremen would have moved on, especially when no one seemed to care about the Leaning R like my great-grandma did."

There was a lot Carly didn't know about Ian, a lot he hadn't shared. And he wasn't sure how much he wanted her to know.

He hadn't just been looking for work when he'd landed the job on the Leaning R, he'd been looking for a place to call home. And the elderly widow hadn't just found a ranch hand and future foreman, she'd found the grandson she'd always hoped Charles would be.

The two had looked after each other until her death. And even when Rosabelle Rayburn was gone and the late Charles Rayburn had taken charge of her estate, Ian had continued to look after her best interests. It soon became clear that Charles hadn't given a rip about the ranch, and if Ian hadn't been there, who knew what would have happened to the Leaning R?

Like Granddad used to say, *You can't buy loyalty, son. But when it's earned and real, it lasts beyond death*. And those words had proven to be true when it came to Rosabelle and the ranch she'd loved.

Ian shrugged. "I don't have anywhere else to go. Besides, I like Brighton Valley. And I plan to settle here and buy a piece of land."

After Charles died and his oldest son, Jason, became the trustee, Jason had announced that he intended to sell the ranch. When Ian heard that, he decided to purchase it himself. He'd developed more than a fondness for the Leaning R, and not just because he'd worked the land. He'd enjoyed all the stories Granny used to tell him about the history of the place, about the rugged Rayburn men who'd once run cattle here.

"I take it you've been putting some money aside," Carly said.

"You could say that."

"If you need any help, let me know. I'd be happy to loan you some." Carly had a trust fund, so she didn't have any financial worries. Apparently, she assumed Ian was little more than a drifter and needed her charity.

"Thanks, but I'll be all right."

It might come as a big surprise to Carly and her brothers—because it certainly had to Ralph Nettles, the Realtor who would be listing the property—but Ian had money stashed away from his days on the road with Felicia. He also had plenty of royalties coming in from the songs he'd written for her.

So, since he could no longer inherit or purchase the Rocking M from his granddad, buying the Leaning R was the next best thing.

"You know that song you were just playing?" Carly asked.

"What about it?"

"Would you sing it for me? From the beginning?"

Ian had written it right after she'd left the ranch the last time, after they'd both come to the decision that it would be best to end things between them. And while Carly had seemed to think their breakup had been permanent, he hadn't been convinced. She usually came running back to the Leaning R whenever life dealt her a blow, so he'd known she'd return—eventually.

Not that he'd expected her to fail. Hell, she had more talent than her mother and—from what Ian had seen and heard—more heart than either of her parents. And he suspected that, deep down, what she really yearned for was someone to love and appreciate her for who she really was.

Ian wasn't sure that he was that man, though.

Then again, he wasn't convinced that he wasn't, either.

He reached for his guitar, then nodded toward the empty chair on the porch, the one she used to sit on during those romantic nights she'd spent with him in his cabin.

Once she was seated beside him, he sang the song he'd written about the two of them, wondering if she'd connect the dots, if she'd guess that she'd inspired the words and music.

When the last guitar chords disappeared into the night, she clapped softly. "That was beautiful, Ian. I love it. But I have to ask you something. Did you write that song about...us?"

"No, not really," he lied. "When you left, I got to thinking about lovers ending a good thing for all the right reasons. And the words and music just seemed to flow out of me. I guess you could say the song almost wrote itself."

He wasn't about to admit that the words had actually come from his heart. He'd become so adept at hiding his feelings, especially from a woman who'd become— or who was about to become—an ex-lover, that it was easier to let the emotion flow through his guitar.

"You really should do something with that song," Carly said. "In the right hands—or with the right voice— it could be a hit."

No one knew that better than Ian. With one phone call to Felicia, the song would strike platinum in no time. But then, before he knew it, every agent and musician in Nashville would be knocking on his door, insisting he come out of retirement and write for them. And there'd go his quiet life and his privacy.

"Would you please let me sing that with you as a duet at the Stagecoach Inn on Saturday night?" Carly lifted the platter of brownies in a tempting fashion. "If you do, I'll leave the rest of these with you."

A smile slid across his face. He'd always found Carly to be tempting, especially when she was determined to have her way. Sometimes he even gave in to her, but this time he couldn't be swayed. "I may have one heck of a sweet tooth, but you can't bribe me with goodies. It won't work."

She blew out a sigh and pulled the platter back. "Don't make me ask Don Calhoun to play for me."

That little weasel? Surely she wasn't serious. "The guy who hit on you that night we stopped at the Filling

Station to have a drink on our way home from the movies in Wexler?"

"Don went to school with me, and we sometimes performed together at the county fair."

Ian clucked his tongue. "Calhoun's a jerk. I saw him watching you from across the room. And as soon as I excused myself to go to the restroom, he took my seat and asked you out."

"Like I said, Don and I are old friends. But if it makes you feel better, I told him no and let him know that you and I were dating."

But they weren't dating anymore. And, old friends or not, the guy was still a tool.

"What's the deal at the Stagecoach Inn on Saturday night?" Ian asked.

"They're having a local talent night. Our gig would just be a few songs—thirty minutes at the most. Will you please sing with me?"

"Now it's playing *and* singing?"

She held out the brownies, offering him the entire plate, and smiled.

But it wasn't the brownies that caused his resolve to waver, it was the beautiful blonde whose bright blue eyes and dimples turned him every which way but loose. He'd had all kinds of women throw themselves at him, and he'd never lost his head, never forgotten that there were some who weren't interested in the real man inside. But there was something about Carly Rayburn that reached deep into the heart of him, something sweet, something vulnerable.

"Damn it, Carly. I'll do it. But just this once."

"Thanks, Ian. You won't regret this."

She was wrong. They were going to have to practice together every evening from now until Saturday. And he was already regretting it.

Chapter Three

Carly couldn't believe how talented Ian was on a guitar—and how good they sounded together. Of course, that hadn't made practicing with him any easier. In fact, over the past few nights, each session seemed to have gotten progressively harder to endure than the last, with this being the most difficult yet.

The air almost crackled with the soaring pheromones, the heady scent of Ian's woodsy cologne and the soft Southern twang of his voice as they performed on the front porch of his cabin. Still, she sang her heart out.

As the music flowed between them, the words of the love songs they'd chosen taunted the raw emotion she'd once felt whenever she'd been in his arms. And it seemed to be truer now than ever, since this was their last chance to practice before singing at the local honky-tonk.

"Let's try 'Breathe' one last time," Ian said. "Then we can call it a night."

"All right," she said, but she feared that if she sang the sexy lyrics of that particular song once more time, she'd refuse to call it a night until she'd kissed the breath right out of her old lover. And then look at the fix she'd be in.

She stole a glance at the handsome cowboy and caught a sparkle in his eyes. The crooked grin tugging at his lips suggested that he knew exactly what he'd done. And that he'd planned all along to suggest the Faith Hill hit as their wrap-up tonight.

Darn him. He probably thought that after singing about the heated desire they shared she'd be more likely to suggest one last night of lovemaking—for old times' sake. But she couldn't do that, even though the idea was sorely tempting.

She had half a notion to scratch that particular song from their list. And she would have done it, too, if they hadn't sounded so good together.

When the song ended, she reached for the glass of water she'd left on the porch railing and took a sip.

"We should be ready for tomorrow night," Ian said, as he placed his guitar back into its case.

Had she been wrong about his intentions?

It appeared so, and while she should be relieved, she tamped down the momentary disappointment.

"Thanks for agreeing to sing with me," she said again.

He didn't respond, which suggested that he still wasn't happy about being forced— No, not forced. She'd only encouraged him. But he'd given his word, which meant he'd follow through on the commitment.

Carly glanced near the front door, at the spot on the wooden flooring where Cheyenne lay curled up asleep. She would have stooped to give the puppy an affectionate pat before leaving, but she hated to wake her.

Instead, she tucked her fingers into the front pocket of her jeans. "I think we're going to knock 'em dead at the Stagecoach Inn."

"You might be right," Ian said, "but keep in mind that it's only a one-shot deal."

That's what they'd agreed to, but she hoped it was actually their first of many performances. She kept that to herself. At this point, there was no need to provoke him any more than she had.

Once he performed with her, she knew the audience would convince him that they were a perfect duo. And then maybe Ian would finally come to the same indisputable conclusion she had—that their amazing chemistry went beyond the bedroom and was destined to light up the stage.

Ian had been in more than his share of honky-tonks during the early days of his career, and the Stagecoach Inn was no different than the others.

Once he crossed the graveled parking lot, climbed the wooden steps and opened the door, the smell of booze and smoke, as well as the sounds of a blaring jukebox and hoots of laughter, slammed into him, taking him back in time to a place he no longer wanted to be.

He stood in the doorway for a moment, watching the people mill about and chatter among themselves.

When he'd been known as Mac McAllister, one of Felicia's Wiley Five, he'd worn his hair long. A bristled face had given him a rugged look he'd favored back then.

Hopefully, no one would recognize him now that he'd shaved and cut his hair in a shorter style. He was also dressed differently, opting for a white button-down shirt and faded jeans, rather than the mostly black attire he'd worn on stage before.

It wasn't until a couple came up behind him that he finally stepped inside the honky-tonk. With his guitar in hand, he made his way across the scarred wood floor to the bar, which stretched across the far wall. In the old days, when he'd played with the Wiley Five, he'd relied on a couple of shots of tequila to get him through the performance. But that wasn't his problem as he headed toward the bar tonight—his throat was just dry.

He was also annoyed at Carly for forcing his hand— or maybe he was just plain angry at himself for rolling over and agreeing to perform with her. He didn't normally do anything he didn't feel like doing.

So why had he agreed to do it for her?

Why here? Why now?

And why had she asked him to meet her here instead of riding over together? Something didn't quite seem right. She might say she hadn't played her daddy, but that wasn't true. And while she might think she could wrap Ian around her little pinky, too, that definitely wasn't the case. After tonight, it wouldn't happen again.

The thirtysomething bartender, a busty brunette in a low-cut tank top, leaned forward across the polished oak bar and offered him an eyeful. "Can I get you a drink, cowboy? It's happy hour. Draft beers are two for one."

"No, thanks. I'm not looking for a deal."

"Ooh. Big spender. I like that in my men."

Ian liked his bartenders to keep quiet and do their job. Instead of serving the patrons, this flirty brunette ought to be seated on the other side of the bar, tempting the male customers to buy her a drink.

"I'll have a root beer," he said.

Her eyes widened, and her lips parted. "Seriously?"

"You got a problem with my order?"

"Nope." She straightened and her smile faded. "Coming right up."

He glanced over his shoulder at the door, wondering where Carly was. He doubted she'd be late. The performance was too important to her.

The busty barkeep set a can and a frosted mug in front of him. "Do you want to run a tab?"

"Nope." He placed a ten dollar bill on the bar, then took a swig of his soda pop.

"That's a shame. I was looking forward to serving you all night."

As the brunette turned to get Ian's change, Carly, who'd apparently just arrived, eased in beside him. She was wearing a brand-new outfit—at least, as far as he could tell. And with her makeup done to a tee, she was just as beautiful as ever, although he preferred to see her without all the hairspray and glitz.

"I'm sorry I'm late," she said.

"I haven't been here long."

She laughed, her eyes sparkling. "I'm just glad you showed up."

Ian reached for her hand and held it tight, his thumb pressing against her wrist, where her pulse rate kicked up a notch. "I said I'd be here, Carly. And while I'll admit I'm not happy about doing it, when I give my word about something, I keep it. So if you had any real doubts, you don't know me as well as you think."

Her glimmering eyes widened, and her lips parted. He wasn't sure if it was his words or his touch setting her emotions reeling. Either way, he didn't mind. There were a few things she needed to get straight about him. He was loyal and honest to a fault. But he wasn't anyone's lapdog.

He released her hand, his own heart rate pulsing through his veins, his own emotions swirling around in a slurpy mess. What was it about Carly Rayburn that set him off like this?

"I'm sorry for pushing you," she said, "but this is going to be fun. You won't be sorry once you see how people react to the two of us singing. Besides, we practiced—and we sound good together."

They had practiced. And they did do well. Carly had a beautiful voice, maybe even better than Felicia's. It had a sultrier edge to it, a sexy, intoxicating sound that the fans were going to eat up. Hell, Ian could listen to her talk or laugh or sing all night long.

"What time are we supposed to go on?" he asked.

"Around nine o'clock—give or take a few minutes. Do you want to find a table? Or would you rather sit here at the bar?"

He glanced at the bartender, who was laying down his change, her eyes and her sullen expression focused on Carly.

"I'd be more comfortable at one of the booths in the corner," he said. "Come on, let's go."

This time, he didn't give her a chance to argue.

Carly followed Ian as he made his way through the crowd to an out-of-the-way spot in the back. She hadn't meant to push him or to anger him. No matter what he might think, she wasn't that type of woman. But in this case, she felt she was doing him a favor.

She supposed she was doing herself one, too.

The only way the two of them could strike up any kind of romantic relationship again, one that might even prove lasting, was if they could perform together. Once they did, he'd see that he was meant to pursue a career in music, same as she. But even then, a commitment might be questionable. Carly was used to strong men. And Ian seemed so…quiet and unassuming. Perhaps he just needed a little push now and then to help build his self-confidence.

She'd struggled with that herself until Braden's mom encouraged her to sing in the Sunday choir one summer. And it had done wonders for her.

Yes, all Ian needed was to see that there was a future for him as a singer and musician—one that was more exciting and profitable than working someone else's cattle for the rest of his life.

Of course, when Ian had grabbed her hand this evening, when he'd admonished her for not trusting him to be a man of his word, he'd certainly given her reason to doubt her initial assessment of him.

Sure, she knew he was a good man, an honest one. And there was no question he was an amazing and considerate lover. She wouldn't have gotten involved with him in the first place if that hadn't been the case. It's just that they'd hit this fork in their road, and he wanted to go a different direction than she did.

She wouldn't claim it hadn't hurt her to end things between them, but it had been for the best. Really.

Now, as they sat in silence in a darkened corner booth, Ian's expression somber, she knew she had to think of something to say, something to change his mood. But before she could give it any thought, a blonde cocktail waitress stopped at their table.

"Can I get y'all a drink?" she asked.

Carly would have ordered a glass of wine, but her tummy had been bothering her again. Not as badly as it had in San Antonio, but she didn't dare risk a bout of nausea before performing. "I'll have a lemon-lime soda."

"You got it." The cocktail waitress looked at Ian and smiled. "How about you?"

"I'll have a shot of tequila—Patrón or the best you have."

Now that was a surprise. Ian never drank—at least, Carly hadn't seen him drink. But apparently, she didn't know him as well as she'd thought.

"I didn't realize you liked tequila," she said.

He didn't respond.

Maybe he was just taking the edge off his nerves. She probably should have been a little more understanding, but there was only one way to kick a little stage fright, and that was to perform right through it.

He remained quiet, his expression intense, until the waitress brought his drink. Carly expected him to grimace at the taste, but instead, he threw it back as if it were the sweet tea he sometimes favored.

Okay, so maybe he hadn't always been the teetotaler she'd thought he might be. But if a stiff shot eased his nerves, that was fine with her.

Fortunately, they didn't have to wait long. Just before nine o'clock, Earl Tellis, the owner of the Stagecoach Inn, took the stage, following two cowboys who played the fiddle.

"Folks, we have a real treat for y'all tonight. Most of you know Rosabelle Rayburn, who owned the Leaning R Ranch and who was one of the finest women in these parts. Well, her great-granddaughter, Carly, and her foreman, Ian, will be singing for you now. Come on up here, you two."

"You ready?" Carly asked as she slid out from the booth.

Ian, who'd corralled his empty shot glass with both hands, grumbled like a bear coming out of his cave in the spring. But like he'd said, he'd given her his word that he'd sing with her tonight.

A rush of guilt and regret swept through her, sending her tummy on a roller-coaster ride. Okay, maybe she shouldn't have pushed him to do something that made him uncomfortable. But it was too late to back-pedal now. So she headed to the stage as Ian joined her, his guitar in hand.

Just as they'd done during their practice sessions on his porch at the ranch, they sang and played their hearts out. And when they were done, the honky-tonk crowd whooped and hollered and cheered.

This wasn't the kind of stage Carly had set her sights on, but it certainly was the audience appreciation she'd hoped for. She glanced at Ian, who simply nodded at the crowd, then returned to his seat at the table.

So much for wishing he'd be inspired by the crowd's reaction.

Carly had no more than reached the booth where they'd been sitting earlier when Earl Tellis joined her and Ian.

"That was amazing. I can't tell you how much I enjoyed hearing you two play and sing. What talent—and you seem to bring out the best in each other."

Carly brightened. She'd felt that same chemistry in Ian's arms as well as on his front porch when they'd sung together. So it was nice to know she wasn't the only one who'd sensed it. "Why, thank you, Earl."

"In fact, I'd like to offer you a job singing here on Friday and Saturday nights."

"That'd be great." Carly glanced at Ian, hoping he'd be as flattered as she was.

"Thanks for the offer," Ian said, "but I'm afraid I'm not interested."

His words slammed into her, and she struggled to get back on an even keel. "Mr. Tellis, why don't you let us talk this over. We'll get back to you."

"There's nothing to talk over," Ian said. "My mind was made up before I even walked in the door."

She'd known that, but she'd hoped he'd feel differently once they got on stage together, once he saw the reaction she'd expected. "Can't you please think about it for a few days? I mean, what would it hurt?"

"I'm a rancher, not a performer." Ian tipped his hat at Earl. "But thanks again for the offer, Mr. Tellis."

Carly crossed her arms. "Well, my mind isn't made up."

"Isn't it?" Ian's gaze grilled into her. "Nobody is stopping you from taking the gig. I wouldn't dream of trying to talk you into doing something you didn't want to do."

Her cheeks flamed with guilt, and she couldn't think of a response, other than another apology, but she doubted that would help at this point.

"I'll see you back at the ranch," he said.

As Ian strode across the floor, Carly turned to Earl. "Give me a day or two. But either way, I might just take the job, even if I have to find another guitarist."

Then she followed Ian outside. She didn't catch up to him until they reached the graveled parking lot.

"I'm sorry for pushing so hard," Carly said to his

back. "But what's the matter with you? I don't get it. You have more talent than anyone I've ever met. You could really go somewhere with that guitar and your voice. Do you know how many people would kill for talent like that?"

Ian slowed to a stop and turned. "I'm not interested in going anywhere. Remember?"

"Yes, but why not? Are you afraid of crowds? Everyone gets a little nervous before performing, but you'll get used to it. I promise."

"Just drop it, Carly. You might have set your sights on a singing career, but I haven't. Can't you get it through your pretty head and one-track brain that I'm perfectly content staying in Brighton Valley?"

"Yes, I know. You told me that. But I can't seem to wrap my mind around it. Not when you're so musically gifted. Have you ever heard yourself play and sing? You're every country girl's dream."

Ian lifted his hat and raked his fingers through his dark hair. "That life isn't for me, Carly. And nothing you can say is going to change my mind."

"You're as stubborn as a mule, Ian McAllister."

He blew out a heavy sigh and shook his head. "You might have been able to wrap your daddy and mama around your little finger—or guilt them into doing whatever you asked. But it won't work with me." Then he turned and headed for his truck.

"Darn it, Ian." She followed after him, speaking to his broad back. "You have no idea what it was like for me as a child. And just for the record, I was never able to guilt anyone into doing squat for me."

When he reached for the door handle, she grabbed his shirtsleeve and gave it a tug. "Would you please wait?"

He turned, and their gazes met. She stroked his muscular forearm, hoping to disarm his irritation. For a moment, passion flared between them, just as it always did whenever she touched him. But this time, her entire body began to buzz, too. Colors merged and Ian's face blurred before her eyes.

Her lips parted, but before she could tell him she felt lightheaded, everything went black.

Ian had never been so angry at a woman in his life. He was about to lay into Carly and tell her so, when her grip on his arm loosened and she uttered a weird sound before slumping to the ground in a dead faint.

What the hell? He stooped and caught her just before her head hit the gravel.

"Carly? Are you all right?" He knelt beside her, holding her close, his heart pounding like crazy. "Honey, talk to me. What's wrong?"

A couple of cowboys wandered past him, heading to the bar. As they spotted him holding a limp Carly, they changed their course and approached him.

"Is she okay?" one asked. "Do you need an ambulance?"

Ian had a cell phone in his pocket, but he'd rather have both hands available to hold her. "Yeah. Would you call 9-1-1?"

He had no idea what was wrong with her. He did know she'd come home from San Antonio with some kind of lingering virus. Or so her brother Jason had told him.

Was it something more serious? Something Carly hadn't wanted him to know?

Ian had no idea, but the thought of losing her, of seeing her hooked up to wires and tubes and…

Okay, slow down. Maybe she'd only fainted. Maybe it was something easily explained, like iron-poor blood.

"Do you know CPR?" the cowboy who wasn't talking on his cell phone asked.

Ian had taken a first-aid course in high school. And while he wasn't an expert, he remembered what he'd learned. But Carly's pulse was strong, her breathing slow but steady. "She doesn't need it."

Not yet, anyway.

The cowboy on his cell disconnected the line, then shoved his phone back in his pocket. "Paramedics are on the way."

By that time, a small crowd had gathered around them. Someone whispered, "That's the pretty little gal who was singing just a few minutes ago. I wonder what happened?"

"Was she hit by a car?" another bystander asked.

"She's probably had too much to drink," the guy next to him said.

Ian didn't bother to set either of them straight. His thoughts were centered on Carly.

When she moaned and lifted her hand to her forehead, he figured that was a good sign. "Honey, are you okay?"

Her eyes flickered opened. She looked at him and blinked a couple of times, as if trying to focus.

What had caused her to pass out? High blood pressure? Low blood sugar? At times like this, Ian wished he'd gone on to medical school like his grandma had hoped he'd do. But first aid, a human biology course in junior college and talking to every nurse or doctor he could corner while seated at his granddad's bedside in the cardiac unit ICU four years ago hadn't made him an expert.

After what seemed like ages, but was probably only a couple of minutes, an ambulance sounded in the distance, causing Carly to become even more aware of her surroundings.

"What…happened?" she asked.

"You passed out." Ian brushed the hair from her forehead and caressed her cheek.

She glanced at the crowd gathered around her, pressing into them.

"Give her some air," Ian told the bystanders.

Carly tried to sit up, but he stopped her. "Just lie here until the paramedics arrive. We'll get you checked out at the medical center, and you'll be fit as a fiddle in no time at all."

She slumped back in his arms. "I was going to call and make a doctor's appointment on Monday morning."

"Yeah, well, now you won't need to do that." Before he could say anything else, the ambulance pulled into the lot, red lights flashing.

The crowd slowly dispersed, giving paramedics room to move in. Ian knew he should give them space to work, too, so he asked one of the cowboys still standing nearby if he could borrow his jacket.

He rolled it up and placed it under Carly's head, then he eased back, but he remained on his knees beside her.

The paramedics, a red-haired man and a brunette woman, moved in to assess their patient. After taking Carly's vitals, the woman asked, "Any chance you could be pregnant?"

The question, the remote possibility, nearly knocked the wind right out of Ian, and while he waited for Carly's response, he thought he might pass out, too.

Chapter Four

*P*regnant?

The very question threw Carly into a tailspin that had nothing to do with her becoming lightheaded before and everything to do with Ian, who was gazing at her, waiting for an answer.

Sure, the thought had crossed her mind a time or two, but she'd never had morning sickness. She'd only been nauseous in the evenings. She'd also had a couple of periods, although they'd been lighter than usual, which was normal for her, considering her gynecological problems. But what difference did that make? Her doctor had told her it was unlikely that she'd ever conceive.

Had that diagnosis been wrong? Could she have conceived a baby during her fling with Ian? Could that be the real cause of her bouts of nausea and not some strange virus?

They'd used protection, but there were nights when their passion had been so hot, when they'd been so desperate for sexual release that they'd become careless once or twice. But she couldn't admit that here—and now.

Still, she had to respond to the unsettling question. She should be completely honest with the paramedics, but she didn't want to deal with a life-altering possibility now. Not in front of a gaping crowd.

And certainly not in front of the man who'd be the baby's father.

So she said, "No, I don't think so."

While the paramedics took her vitals, Ian got to his feet and took a step back, allowing them room to work. But he remained beside her, waiting, watching. *Listening.*

The brunette medic kneeling beside Carly pulled the stethoscope from her ears. "Everything appears to be normal, but it might be a good idea for us to take you to the hospital just to be sure. The doctors may want to run some tests."

A pregnancy test would probably be the first one on the list, but Carly couldn't deal with that thought tonight.

"I'm feeling better now," she said. "I'd rather just go home and take it easy. I'll call my doctor first thing on Monday morning and make an appointment to see her."

Ian eased closer. "Carly, I'd rather you go to the ER tonight and get checked out."

Was he concerned about her health—or eager to hear if she was pregnant? She wanted to have that test, too, so she could rule it out.

Or wrap her mind around the possibility.

The more she thought about it, the more plausible it seemed—in spite of what her doctor had said. But if she was pregnant, she'd be…what? Four months along? Why, that was nearly halfway there…

She fought a flash of panic and the urge to place her hand on her tummy, where she'd noticed that she'd put on weight. She'd blamed it on her hormonal imbalance. But had she been wrong?

She scanned the faces of the strangers who'd gathered around her.

This couldn't be happening.

Think, girl. Think.

"I'm sure it isn't anything serious." She sat up, hoping her head didn't start spinning again. But shoot, just thinking about—

Oh, for Pete's sake. She was making way too much out of this. A doctor had given her every reason to believe that it was unlikely she would ever be able to have a baby. Besides, she and Ian had used contraceptives, so surely there wasn't a chance of pregnancy. At least, she hoped not.

Carly blew out a sigh and looked at Ian. "I'm fine. I didn't have much for lunch, so I probably just need to eat something."

He studied her, questioning her with a gaze so intense that she felt herself start to unravel.

To be honest, she wasn't sure about anything right

now, but she didn't want him to worry—or worse, have any doubts about the truth of her response.

"I'm sure a juicy hamburger will do the trick." She offered him a wobbly smile, although the thought of a greasy burger suddenly turned her stomach.

The crowd, no doubt realizing her fainting spell was minor and that there'd be more excitement inside the honky-tonk, began to disperse. And the paramedics packed up their gear.

The only one who didn't seem convinced that the crisis was over was Ian.

Concern and suspicion swirled in Ian's head, at odds with each other. Carly might say that she couldn't be pregnant, but why had she fainted? Was it just a troubling stomach bug?

If she was pregnant and the baby was Ian's, she'd have to be about four months along. But then again, she could have met someone else while she was away, someone who'd broken her heart and caused her to quit the show and run home to the Leaning R.

The realization that she might have found another guy so quickly didn't sit very well and gnawed at him for more reasons than one.

After he and Felicia Jamison had become lovers, things had been good between them for a while. But then Felicia had gotten pregnant. Ian had been stunned, yet pleased at the prospect of becoming a father. But she'd chosen to have an abortion rather than have their baby, saying that a child would sidetrack her booming career.

Ian had always wanted a family of his own, so he'd been crushed by her decision. And that's when the bright lights and glamour of touring and performing onstage began to fade.

His and Felicia's relationship had faded at that point, too. And she soon moved on to someone else.

Ian hadn't been all that bothered by their breakup, though. The fact that Felicia had cared so little about the baby they'd created told him how she felt about their relationship—and about him.

Splitting up had actually been for the best. He wanted more out of a lifetime partner, more out of a wife.

He reached out to Carly and helped her to her feet. "Then let's go home. We'll take my pickup. You can leave yours here, and I'll bring you back to get it in the morning."

He half expected her to object, since they didn't always see things eye to eye, but she said, "All right."

"And on the way home," he added, "I'll get you that juicy burger."

"Sounds good. Thanks." She followed him to his Dodge Ram. When he opened the passenger door, she slid onto the seat.

The drive to Burger Junction only took five minutes, yet neither of them spoke on the way.

Was Carly still feeling the effects of her fainting spell? Or was she thinking about what might really be wrong with her? His curiosity, as well as the silence in the cab, grew until he thought he'd go crazy.

"Do you want to order takeout or go inside and eat?" he asked.

"Actually, I'd rather eat at home—if you don't mind."

"Not at all."

They pulled into the drive-through and placed their orders. When they finally headed back to the ranch, Ian's suspicion had built to the point that it was all he could think of.

He stole a glance at her and watched as she stared out the window and into the night.

"So you don't think you could be pregnant?" he asked.

She bit down on her bottom lip, as though pondering the question—or even the possibility. Then she turned to him. "I don't see how. I mean, we used condoms."

Did that mean he was the only possible father?

"They aren't a hundred percent effective," he said.

"I know, but I doubt I'm pregnant." She offered him a breezy smile that didn't do much to reassure him.

"Maybe we should stop by the all-night drugstore in Wexler and pick up a pregnancy test."

"We don't need to do that. I'd rather wait and see what the doctor has to say on Monday."

She hadn't given him any reason to think that she'd been with someone else. Not that he could object since they'd ended things between them. It's just that he hadn't felt the need to find another lover.

Not yet, anyway.

Still, after what he and Felicia had gone through, Ian wasn't sure he wanted to face something similar again.

Damn. That's all he needed—Carly pregnant with his baby, yet hell-bent on being a star.

Then again, she'd said she didn't think it was possible. And at this point, he had no reason to doubt her.

True to his word, Ian took Carly to get her pickup at the Stagecoach Inn on Saturday morning. To ease the awkwardness and to avoid discussing her potential health issue, Carly focused their conversation on safe subjects like the weather and the long-forgotten items in Granny's attic that still needed to be sorted through and packed away.

As soon as they arrived at the honky-tonk, she slid out of the truck, grabbed her purse and thanked him for the ride.

"No problem." He studied her again, his left arm draped over the steering wheel, his expression unreadable. "I'll follow you back to the ranch."

And face his scrutiny again? She'd be a basket case within an hour. "You go on ahead. I have some errands to run in Wexler, so I'll see you later."

To be honest, even if she didn't have a single thing on her to-do list, she planned to make herself scarce today. She had to escape the intensity in his gaze, which reached deep inside of her, making her question every word she'd ever said, anything she'd ever done and each emotion she'd ever felt. So she would stay away from the ranch until late that evening.

But first she had a very important stop to make.

Ian had suggested it last night on the way home from the Stagecoach Inn, but she'd refused to even consider it then. He was the last person she wanted with her when she purchased a home pregnancy test. But now that she was on her own, she could hardly wait to buy one and see what it had to say.

Fifteen minutes later, she pulled into the parking lot of the largest drugstore in Wexler. Then she slipped on a pair of sunglasses, hoping to avoid being recognized by anyone who might possibly know her, and headed for the entrance.

She'd be darned if she was going to get into the checkout lane with only one item in her hand, particularly a pregnancy test, so she grabbed a small red basket, hung the handle over her arm, and walked up and down the aisles until she'd filled it with stuff she really didn't need.

Along the way, she picked up a box of chocolates, peach-scented lotion and a get-well card for Braden's grandpa. She added deodorant, toothpaste and tampons, which she thought was a clever way to throw off suspicion. Then she headed for the shelves that held her primary reason for the shopping venture and snatched the first box she spotted, not taking the time to read the claims or directions on the box.

As nonchalantly as she could, she made her way to the checkout lanes.

If the clerk at the register thought anything strange about her purchase, she didn't blink an eye. Instead, she tallied the total and waited for Carly to count out the cash.

Moments later, Carly was out the door and pondering her next step. She could wait until she was at home tonight and in the privacy of her own room to take the test, but she'd probably die of anticipation in the meantime.

But where should she go?

As she climbed into her truck, she noticed a fast food restaurant to the right—Billy Bob's Burgers. They'd have a public restroom inside, which made the ordeal feel pretty clandestine. But that seemed like the best option since she didn't want to wait another minute.

She parked near the entrance, went inside and placed an order for a breakfast burrito and an orange juice. Then she headed for the ladies' room and chose a stall.

Her fingers trembled as she took the box from her purse, tore into it and read the instructions. After following the directions, she placed the small, plastic apparatus on top of a folded paper towel, then set it on the shelf where she'd left her purse and waited. Apparently, it was supposed to take several minutes for a positive line to show up, but the answer formed almost immediately.

She blinked twice, hoping to get a better read, but there was no doubting the results.

Pregnant.

As the line brightened like a neon sign, her heart raced. That couldn't be right. Could it? Dr. Connor had told her it wasn't likely that she'd ever conceive. But the plastic apparatus on the shelf argued otherwise.

The doctor had been wrong.

Or was it the test? Maybe it was a false positive.

The door to the restroom opened and closed, indicating someone else had come in. Carly needed to get out of here, but she couldn't seem to make her feet work.

She was…*pregnant*? She wasn't sure if she should laugh or cry. She supposed she'd get used to the idea with time. But if she was actually going to have a baby, what in the world would she tell Ian?

Somehow Carly stumbled through the morning. She'd managed to drink her juice, but she'd yet to remove her breakfast burrito from the bag. Apparently, the results of the pregnancy test had stolen her appetite.

She was still determined to avoid going home so she didn't have to face Ian, who deserved to know the truth. But until she was able to wrap her own mind around the news and figure out some sort of game plan, she wasn't ready to tell him anything.

For that reason, she'd gone window shopping on Wexler Boulevard. She was studying a bright red dress on a blonde mannequin in the window of the new women's shop that opened recently when her cell phone rang. She pulled the iPhone from her purse and glanced at the display.

She didn't feel like talking to anyone, but her mother didn't call often, so she probably ought to take it. If Carly had a normal mom, she might be tempted to share her news—or rather, her confusion. But Carly and Raelynn had never had that kind of relationship.

"Hey, there," Carly said. "How's it going, Raelynn?"

The country singer turned oilman's wife paused for a beat. "You know, darlin', it's okay now for you to call me Mom or Mama."

Maybe so, but old habits were hard to break.

And relationships were what they were.

"How's David?" Carly asked. Her mother had fallen hard for her second husband, hard enough to give up her singing career. Or maybe she just yearned for another spotlight these days—the wife of a bigwig senator.

"He's doing fine—and gearing up for reelection. So we've had a slew of dinner parties and fundraisers to attend. Thankfully, we're flying to London later on this month, which will be a nice break. But I called to check on *you*."

That was nice—yet a little unexpected.

"I was in San Antonio last night with some friends," Raelynn added, "and we tried to attend your show."

That was an even bigger surprise. Raelynn usually hadn't found the time to attend any of Carly's performances before—even when she'd been a child in school.

"The director told me you'd gotten sick and quit," Raelynn added. "What happened? And where are you?"

Her mother's concern touched her, yet she wasn't about to go into detail. "I got a persistent case of the stomach flu and had to leave the show. I've been staying at the Leaning R."

"Are you feeling better now?"

"Yes, I am. Thanks." But the revelation of another diagnosis was on the horizon, one Carly doubted her mother could possibly be prepared for. She'd just given Carly permission to call her Mom, but how would she feel about someone calling her Grandma?

"You know," Raelynn said, her voice lacking the Southern twang that had been her trademark on the stage. "You're always welcome to come to Houston and stay with David and me. We have plenty of room. You can even housesit while we're gone."

While she appreciated the offer, that was out of the question. It wasn't that Carly didn't like Senator David Crowder. He was as charming as her father had been— maybe even more so. Nor had she held on to a childish wish that her parents had stayed together. They really hadn't been suited.

But Carly had never been comfortable staying at her stepfather's house. Not that she'd felt truly at home in Raelynn's elegant townhouse prior to their marriage, either.

"Thanks for the offer," Carly said, "but I'm helping Jason inventory Granny's belongings." That was true, of course. And the best reason to give her mother. She might not have ever been especially close to Raelynn, but there was no reason to hurt her feelings.

"How is your brother?" Raelynn asked. "I'll bet he's been busy since Charles died. He's in charge of the estate, isn't he?"

"Yes, and he's fine. He married Juliana Bailey, an old friend of mine, last weekend. They're on their honeymoon."

"I don't remember her."

Why would she? Raelynn had been on tour so often that she'd scarcely remembered she even had a daughter.

"Juliana grew up on a ranch here in Brighton Valley," Carly said. "She and I used to ride horses together whenever I stayed with Granny at the Leaning R."

"So where did Jason take his new bride?" Raelynn asked.

"To Mexico." Carly wasn't going to tell her mother about the family mystery or how Braden had learned their father had been looking for a woman named Camilla Cruz when he'd died down in that car accident six months ago.

When Braden learned this his grandfather was ill, he had to return home, but not before finding out Camilla had died and that her two young children had been placed in an orphanage. So Jason and his new bride had continued the search for the kids.

"You'd think Jason could be more imaginative and take his wife to Tahiti or to Paris—somewhere romantic. But then again, when it really mattered, your father wasn't very romantic, either."

Carly let the comment go unchallenged and tried to come up with another topic.

Raelynn gave a little snort. "I always feared that boy would grow up just like Charles. Now he's dragged his new wife on a business trip and he's masking it as a honeymoon."

That wasn't true. Jason told Carly he planned to take Juliana on a real honeymoon once they located Camilla's children. But there was no need to defend him at this point. The truth would come out one of these days.

Raelynn had falsely assumed that Charles had been in Mexico, working on some big business venture,

when he'd had that accident. And it was just as well
that she did. She had a tendency to repeat tales, but not
before adding a little to them.

Besides, Raelynn had always had hard feelings toward Charles after their split. In fact, their divorce had
taken several years to settle. Too bad their courtship
hadn't lasted long enough for them to realize just how
ill-suited they were and saved each other the trouble.

Carly had only been eight at the time, but she didn't
remember being too affected by their breakup. She
hadn't seen much of either parent when they'd been
together. As a result, she'd grown up in their shadows. Was it any wonder she wanted to break free and
do something on her own?

"Well, I suppose I'd better let you go," Raelynn said.
"I have a hair appointment at eleven, then a lunch date
with Claire, Senator Dobson's wife."

"Have fun."

"How about you?" Raelynn asked. "Do you have
any special plans today?"

"No. Nothing out of the ordinary."

In fact, the only thing she had going on in the near
future was figuring out a way to break the news to Ian
that he was going to be a father.

And making an appointment on Monday with the
woman who'd been Carly's gynecologist before opening a family medical practice. The doctor who'd told
her it wasn't likely that she'd ever get pregnant.

Bright and early Monday morning, at least as far as
Carly was concerned, she called Dr. Selena Connor's

office. After she told the receptionist about the positive pregnancy test and her fainting spell, the woman asked when she'd had her last period.

"I'll have to check my calendar, since I've had a couple of light ones lately, but if you're trying to figure out how far along I am, I can't possibly be less than four months."

"Have you had any prenatal care?" the woman asked.

"I only learned that I was pregnant yesterday," Carly said. "Unless those home tests aren't accurate."

"You'd be more apt to get a false negative," the receptionist said. "Let's get you in here as soon as possible." After a slight pause, she added, "Dr. Connor is going on a short vacation, starting tomorrow, but we can squeeze you in at two o'clock this afternoon. Will that work?"

So soon? Everything seemed to be happening at record speed. And instead of waiting nine months for a baby, she'd only have to wait five.

"That'll be fine. I'll see you then."

With that call out of the way, Carly made a cup of herbal tea. She'd just buttered a toasted English muffin when Ian knocked at the back door.

"Come on in," she called to him.

He entered the kitchen through the mudroom, Cheyenne tagging along behind him, panting as her short legs tried to keep up. He stood with his hat in hand, a slight furrow in his brow. "Good morning. How are you feeling?"

She offered him a smile. "I'm fine." But then again, with the handsome cowboy's eyes caressing her, taunt-

ing her—and yes, questioning the truth of her answer—
she was feeling all kinds of things that could make her
lightheaded enough to swoon.

"Did you get that doctor's appointment?" he asked.

"Yes, I did. It's at two o'clock this afternoon."

"Would you like me to take you?"

No way. Not when she knew that he'd pressure her
to find out what she'd already learned. When she told
him, she wanted to be prepared for his reaction—and
any questions he might have about the future.

"Thanks," she said, "but I'll drive myself."

When he cocked his head, as if doubting her decision, she added, "I'll be okay."

"I'm not so sure about that."

Really. Couldn't he just let it go? The last thing she
needed was to have him sitting with her in the waiting room. Of course, she might be sorry she'd declined
his offer, which actually had been sweet, if Dr. Connor
gave her bad news or a startling, unexpected diagnosis.

Ian continued to study her, his gaze picking at loose
threads in her heart.

Shaking his inspection, which was sure to unravel
her, she asked, "Can I fix you coffee—or maybe an
English muffin?"

"No, thanks. I ate a couple of hours ago."

Of course he had. His days always began at the
crack of dawn, and she was a night owl. In fact, when
they'd been a couple and sleeping together, he'd always
slipped out of bed quietly, not wanting to wake her.

A mental picture of the two of them in bed began to
form in her mind. But this time they weren't sleeping.

Ian had been a considerate lover. An amazingly good one, too. But there was more to life than sex.

Yet as his musk and leather scent taunted her and attraction sparked between them, she wasn't so sure about that.

Ian, on the other hand, merely slipped on his hat, turned for the door and strode out of the house with a sexy cowboy swagger, the little wannabe cattle dog bounding out behind him.

Okay, she had to admit that in the scheme of things great sex had its perks and should never be underrated. But she couldn't stew about that now. Not without complicating her life all over again.

For the next hour, Carly went over the inventory list Juliana had left behind. After realizing that it wasn't just the attic that was untouched, but that no one had even begun to pack the basement yet, she turned on the light and headed downstairs. Then she got busy assessing the various antiques and the boxes the Rayburn family had been storing for a couple of generations.

Only trouble was, she hadn't been able to focus on anything other than what the doctor might say this afternoon. So, rather than waste her energy, she returned upstairs, took a shower and headed into town early.

Since she had plenty of time to kill, she drove through Hamburger Junction and ordered a grilled chicken sandwich and a drink. Then she went to the office building next to the Brighton Valley Medical Center, parked under the shade of an elm and tried to force herself to eat something even though her tummy was jumbled.

At one thirty, she walked across the parking lot to the redbrick building that housed various doctors' offices. Once inside the lobby, she took the elevator to the second floor, where Selena Connor practiced family medicine in room 204.

As Carly stepped out the elevator doors, she spotted Shannon Miller, Braden's mother, standing outside another physician's office, next to a man wearing a light blue dress shirt and a stylish tie. The white lab coat he wore suggested he was a doctor.

She'd always liked Braden's mom, who'd gotten pregnant by Carly's dad right after she'd graduated from high school. The wealthy businessman had charmed the young woman into an affair while he was still married to Jason's mom.

Of course, Carly hadn't been born when it happened, but she'd heard the whispers ever since. Apparently it had been quite the town scandal.

When Shannon, whose eyes were red-rimmed, spotted Carly exiting the elevator, she waved her over and introduced her to Dr. Erik Chandler, saying he was an "old friend."

Carly greeted the doctor, then turned to Shannon. "I was sorry to hear that your father isn't doing well."

Shannon tucked a strand of brown hair behind her ear. "It's been tough. The hospice nurse said she couldn't be sure, but she thinks he only has a week or two left. But his affairs are in order. So at least that's one less thing for Braden and me to stress about."

Dr. Chandler placed a comforting hand on Shannon's back. "I need to get back to my patients, but I'll stop by the house this evening."

She offered the man a smile that made her look younger than her forty-six years. "Thank you, Erik. I don't know what I'd do without you."

The handsome doctor cupped her cheek. "You're one of the strongest women I know, Shannon. I'll see you later." Then he headed down the hall.

When a door shut behind them, Shannon said, "Erik and I dated for a while in high school, then he left for college. He's only recently come back to town, but he's been very supportive and helpful. A real blessing, actually."

Carly could understand that, even though the doctor had been right—Shannon was strong. She'd raised Braden on her own, in spite of the town-wide rumors calling her a home wrecker.

After Carly's parents had divorced, Carly had spent summers and holidays at the Leaning R with Granny. She couldn't remember how many times Shannon would invite her over to hang out with Braden. And at Christmas, she always bought presents for both Carly and Jason.

Looking back, Carly suspected that Shannon had felt sorry for her. And in a sense, maybe she'd had reason to. As a child, Carly had been lonely much of the time.

"Braden said you were back in town," Shannon said, "and that you'd gotten sick and had to quit that show in San Antonio. I hope it isn't serious."

It wasn't, at least not in the way Shannon was implying. But the diagnosis was pretty unsettling, especially when Carly had expected an entirely different future for herself.

"I'm just here for a checkup," she said.

"That's good. I know how badly you want to perform. It's all you used to talk about when you were younger."

As a child, Carly had taken music and dance lessons, finding that she had a talent that surpassed her mother's. She'd even gone to an impressive college of performing arts. Yet about the time her mother could have introduced her to the stage and given her a leg up, she'd married David Crowder, a state politician, and retired. Still, Carly had set out to become the country-western star her mother once was.

"I still have that dream," Carly said. "And I intend to make it happen."

"I'm sure you will." Shannon glanced at the elevator. "Well, I'd better go. I need to check on my dad, and I don't want you to be late for your appointment."

"Take care," Carly said. "And please call me if there's anything I can do."

"Thanks, honey. I will."

Then they each turned to go their own way.

Once inside the waiting room, Carly signed in and then took a seat. Thanks to her chat with Shannon, she wasn't nearly as early as she thought she'd be. Her name was called in just a few minutes.

After a stop at the scale, Carly was taken to an exam

room. She didn't have to wait long for Dr. Selena Connor to enter.

"What seems to be the problem?" the pretty brunette asked.

Carly told her about the fainting spell, the evening bouts of nausea and the positive pregnancy test. "I'm not the kind who would ignore those symptoms for so long, but I had some light periods and I wasn't nauseous in the mornings."

"All women are different, and the symptoms can vary. Some aren't even sick at all."

"I told myself there were a zillion reasons I couldn't be pregnant. For one thing, you told me it wasn't likely. Plus we used protection." She placed her hand on her stomach, felt the small bulge that she'd blamed on that dumb hormonal imbalance and bloating.

A small part of her—the little girl who'd once played with dollies and dreamed of being a mommy someday—perked up. But she did her best to shake it off.

After witnessing the disaster of her parents' marriage and divorce, she'd learned not to trust those happy-ever-after urges, and as a result, she'd focused on having a successful career instead.

Still, she'd imagined that she'd have a family someday, an adopted one. But not until her career was going strong.

"I can't believe this," Carly said. "And if you check your notes, you'll see that it wasn't supposed to happen."

The doctor didn't even look at the chart. "Yes, I remember saying it wasn't likely. But I also told you it wasn't impossible."

Carly's heart thumped in both fear and anticipation. That little girl rose up again, and she wondered what it might be like to have a child grow inside her womb, to feel it move and kick.

But could she do right by her son or daughter? Could she overcome her own limited mothering to become a good and loving one herself?

"Why don't you lie back and let me examine you," Dr. Connor said.

Carly complied, stretching out. She stared at the ceiling, afraid to speak, afraid to breathe.

The doctor had hardly palpated Carly's belly when she said, "Your uterus is definitely enlarged."

Carly draped a hand across her eyes. "So it's true. I'm pregnant."

After further examination, the doctor replied, "About four months, from what I can tell, although we'll need to do a sonogram to know for sure. I'm running a very tight schedule today, so I'd like to make an appointment for you to come back for that. I'll also have the nurse provide you with prenatal vitamins and some reading material to answer your questions. In the meantime, you will need some lab work, so we'll have your blood drawn today, too."

Carly nodded. "No problem."

But that wasn't true. It was a huge problem. One she'd have to figure out how to share with Ian.

Chapter Five

Ian lifted his Stetson to cool his sweat-dampened hair. He glanced down the long, graveled driveway that led to the Leaning R, then wiped his brow. A light breeze had finally kicked up, providing a respite from the heat.

All afternoon, the summer sun had been beating down on him while he was hoeing weeds around the yard. But he kept a steady pace, determined not to let up. To his right, Cheyenne had curled up to sleep on a patch of grass in the shade of a maple tree, exhausted from chasing butterflies.

It hadn't been difficult to find chores to do that would keep him close to the house while Carly was in town at the doctor's office. She might have told him that she was feeling much better, but that didn't keep him from worrying about her and wondering what she'd found out.

He stretched out the kinks in his back. He'd gotten quite a workout from his labor and was just about to call it a day when he finally spotted her pickup heading down the drive. So he leaned on the hoe and waited for her to park.

As she climbed from the cab, he asked, "What did the doctor say?"

She reached across the seat for her purse. "It's nothing to worry about." She closed the driver's door, then tossed him an unconvincing smile.

When she didn't offer any more than that, he decided to prod her a bit.

"Are you pregnant?" he asked, focusing on her eyes instead of allowing his gaze to drop to her waistline.

She flushed, then glanced at her feet for a moment. When she looked back at him, she said, "I told you that wasn't likely. Remember?"

Yes, she'd mentioned that on Saturday night. Is that what the doctor had told her again today?

The breeze blew a strand of hair across her face, and she swiped it away.

"I'll tell you what," she said. "Give me time to make a phone call, whip up a salad and make a pot of spaghetti. Then come to the house and have dinner with me. I'll give you more details about my visit to the doctor then."

So what was that supposed to mean? That her diagnosis was long and complex?

Ian's mind swirled with all the possibilities, none of which were the least bit comforting.

"Okay," he said. "Spaghetti sounds good. How much time do you need? An hour?"

"Sure. That works." Then she headed for the back door.

As he watched her go, he continued to lean on the hoe. Her voice and tone had sounded normal. Yet her shoulders slumped.

In defeat? In worry?

Damn. He didn't like waiting. Didn't like stressing about what she might say.

Was she going to drop a bomb about her health? Or was she trying to concoct a believable story meant to not worry him, to not involve him?

Carly had never lied or deceived him before.

So why was he so skeptical now?

Carly had wanted to lie to Ian. And she'd nearly done so. Well, not outright. But the noncommittal response she'd given him was just as dishonest as if she'd come right out and told him she wasn't pregnant. And for that reason, she felt as guilty as sin.

But Dr. Connor had verified her positive test results, which had nearly blown her away. The news had her torn between feeling completely unbalanced and utterly delighted.

How could she share it with Ian when she could hardly fathom it herself?

She entered the kitchen, taking time to run her gaze over the scarred but familiar oak table and chairs, where she used to tell Granny her deepest troubles and secrets. Then she scanned the various plaques, pictures and cross-stitch hangings with upbeat sayings that adorned the walls.

This room had always been a haven for her. She only wished her great-grandma was still here to tell her everything would be fine, that things would work out just the way they were supposed to.

Why couldn't she grasp that reassuring thought now?

She set her purse on the countertop next to the old-style, wall-mounted telephone.

Braden had called her while she'd been at the clinic and had her cell turned off. She'd tried to return his call on the drive back to the ranch, but he hadn't been free to talk to her then. He did, however, say that their brother Jason had called him from Mexico. So she was eager to hear the latest news.

Last month, Braden uncovered the fact that their dad had been searching for a woman named Camilla Cruz, whose father had once been the foreman on the Leaning R. Camilla was an artist who'd died of breast cancer two years ago. No one knew much about her—or why she didn't go by her father's last name of Montoya. But they suspected she'd once been married.

Their father had gone so far as to hire a private investigator to help him find her. He had to have learned that Camilla had passed away, so Carly and her brothers couldn't understand why he'd continued to search for some of Camilla's shirttail relatives.

Then, a couple weeks ago, they'd had a small breakthrough. Jason had found some of her paintings and other artwork in a storage shed their father had rented, indicating their dad had gotten involved in an art import business of some kind. He also discovered some private letters that revealed their father and Camilla had been romantically involved at one time.

Braden had gone to Mexico to follow a lead, and right before he had to return home because of his grandfather's illness, he'd learned that Camilla had two children—a boy and a girl who'd been placed in an orphanage.

Carly wondered if the kids could be their father's, given his past, but it was unlikely. He'd never kept his relationships secret, and since neither of her brothers had a clue that he'd been involved with the artist, they suspected the whole thing must have blown over before it had a chance to take off.

During a family meeting, Carly and her brothers had agreed that the search for those kids should continue. They believed that their father, who'd been a big supporter of the Boys Club and various organizations that benefitted children, had probably been looking for Camilla's son and daughter so he could rescue them and find them a decent home.

Jason and his new bride had taken up the search at that point. In the meantime, Braden was trying to find someone who might be willing to adopt Camilla's children here in the States.

Carly blew out a sigh. She hoped Jason and Juliana would find them. And that they'd make sure the siblings were happy, healthy and safe.

Yet it was her own dilemma, her own burden that weighed her down now. And she felt as if she'd just chugged down a cocktail of surprise, delight and fear.

She was *pregnant*. With Ian's baby.

She'd like nothing better than to cling to her secret for a while longer, to allow it to settle over her so she could come up with a game plan. But Ian wasn't about to let his curiosity rest.

Besides, she'd have to tell him. She was four months along, and soon her baby bump would reveal the truth.

How would the news affect him?

She suspected that he still carried a torch for her. Not that she didn't care for him, too. The man was everything her father wasn't—honest, dependable, trustworthy. And Ian would undoubtedly make a good dad.

But what about her? Would she make a good mom?

Unlike her own mother, she would never go on tours and leave her child in the care of a nanny. She'd take the baby on the road with her.

But while she thought of Ian as a go-with-the-flow kind of guy, she had a feeling that he'd have some very strong opinions about that particular plan.

The unexpected news, the unsettling news, was sure to complicate her life.

And what about Ian? She suspected he would want to be a part of the baby's life. But he'd made it clear several times that he was determined to be a rancher.

And he'd be a good one.

Many years ago, Granny had hired Reuben Montoya as the Leaning R foreman, and he'd done a great job. But about three years ago, he'd been called home for a family emergency and returned to his hometown, a small village located somewhere near the coast in Baja California.

Granny had gone through several different foremen but none of them had worked out—nor had they been able to match the job Reuben had done.

Then she'd met Ian at Caroline's Diner, taken him home and given him a try. From what she'd said several times, Ian had worked out like a charm.

"That boy's got an inborn skill at ranching," Granny had said. "And he has a way with sick and injured critters that's pert near better than any vet I've ever seen."

So it was no surprise that Ian wanted to have his own spread one day. But there lay the biggest hurdle of all. Carly had dreams to reach the sky, and Ian had his boots firmly planted in the Brighton Valley soil.

So how would an unplanned pregnancy fit into either of their lives?

Once Ian learned about the baby, he might try to convince her to stay on the Leaning R and live the humble life of a cowboy's wife forever. And if Carly agreed to something like that, she feared she'd wither and die.

Okay, so he hadn't exactly given her reason to believe that he'd actually want to marry her. But it did seem like the kind of thing that noble Ian would offer.

And marriage was out of the question, especially if it meant giving up her dream.

Of course, she wasn't exactly sure how motherhood would play into her plans for the future. If she was entirely honest, she'd admit she actually could envision herself rocking a baby on the porch, taking a toddler to pick huckleberries in the hills and even baking and decorating sugar cookies from Granny's recipe box with her little one. But living a life of obscurity, like the one Ian had chosen, wasn't an option. There was no way she could possibly live both a vision and a dream.

Still unable to plot a course of action, she moved about the kitchen to fix the dinner Ian would soon come to eat, the dinner at which she'd have to tell him what she'd learned today.

She'd just put the pasta into boiling water when the house phone rang. She wiped her hands on the apron she wore and hurried to answer before the caller hung up.

It was Jason.

"Hey," she said. "How's it going?"

"Romantically speaking, I've never been happier."

"I'm glad to hear that," she said. Jason had been a lone wolf all his life—or for as long as she'd known him. So that was good news indeed. "What about Camilla's kids? Have you located them yet?"

"No, but we've learned that they're seven-year-old twins. After their mother died, they moved in with Reuben, their grandfather, but he passed away last summer. Since that's about the time Dad hired the private investigator, we think his death may have somehow triggered Dad's search."

"So what happened to the kids when their grandfather died?"

"That's where the orphanage comes in to play. We actually found it, but the kids were only there for a few months. They've been staying in the care of a nanny Dad hired."

"Wow." The whole story was growing more mysterious. "Where's the nanny? And what do you know about her?"

"Just her name. We're going to try to find her next. I hope it won't take too long. I really need to head back to the corporate office in Houston soon. Rayburn Energy has an important stockholders' meeting soon, and as CEO, I should attend."

"I understand." Her older brother not only had his own company to run, but he was in charge of their father's family trust and his corporate holdings, too.

She hoped Jason wouldn't expect her to take up the search next. She couldn't speak Spanish, so she'd be lost in Mexico.

No, she'd better stay here on the Leaning R until she figured out her next move.

After taking a long, hot shower to soak his aching muscles and giving himself a fresh shave, Ian turned Cheyenne out to do her doggy business, then left her in the cabin.

The pup whimpered in complaint, and he paused at the door and spoke to her. "Take it easy, girl. I'll be back later."

Cheyenne let out a howl, clearly not understanding that she could trust him to return. But that was something she'd have to learn.

He closed the door, then crossed the yard and arrived at the ranch house, braced to hear what Carly had to say. When he reached the back door, he stood on the porch for a moment, then lifted his hand and knocked.

"Come on in," she called out.

He made his way through the mudroom and into the kitchen, where the aroma of tomatoes, garlic and Italian spices filled the air.

"Dinner is ready," Carly said. "All I have to do is put it on the table."

"It smells great. Can I help?"

"Thanks, but I have everything under control."

Moments later, they were seated across from each other at Granny's antique oak table, preparing to eat.

Ian glanced at the large serving of sauce-covered pasta on his plate, his thoughts as tangled as the strands of spaghetti.

"So what's the deal?" he finally asked.

"Well, I…" Carly sucked in a deep breath, then slowly let it out. "I have a confession to make. I wasn't completely honest with you earlier. It's just that I'm having trouble believing it myself."

"You mean you're *not* fine?" He set down his fork, unable to eat in spite of his hunger, and merely stared at her. "What did the doctor say?"

"No, I'm okay. It's just that…" She worried her bottom lip. "I guess there's no easy way to say it. I'm pregnant, Ian."

He pushed his plate aside, no longer able to eat. "I asked you that an hour ago, and you said—"

"I know. I implied that it wasn't likely. But that's what I was told a couple years ago. Apparently, it wasn't impossible. Dr. Connor confirmed it today. I somehow got pregnant in spite of the odds. And I misread the symptoms, thinking that there was no way I could be."

Ian and Carly hadn't made love in ages—four or five months, to be precise. So he asked the logical question. "Who's the father?"

She stiffened. "You are, you big jerk."

He hadn't meant to offend her. "I'm sorry, Carly. It's just that you'd have to be pretty far along."

"According to Dr. Connor, I'm about four months."

He fought the urge to look at her belly, to see if he could detect a bump. Wouldn't she be showing?

Finally he said, "I'm at a loss for words."

"Imagine how I felt when the doctor confirmed it."

Had she been upset by the news? Shocked to learn she was confronting the same crisis Felicia had once faced?

When Felicia had announced that she was expecting Ian's child, he'd taken it in stride. In fact, he hadn't minded the idea of becoming a father. But it hadn't panned out that way. And he'd been left to grieve for the child he would never meet. But this was different.

Carly was different. And there was something about knowing they'd conceived a baby together that… delighted him.

But what if she decided that a child wasn't in her future, just as Felicia had done?

"So what do you plan to do?" he asked.

She tugged on a strand of hair, then twirled a curl around her finger. "I'm not sure."

He felt compelled to offer to marry her, to promise to be there for her and the baby for the rest of his life. It was, after all, the right thing to do. But, knowing Carly and the big dreams she had, he didn't think it was a good idea to put too much pressure on her when she was just getting used to the idea of expecting their child.

It was too late for an abortion, wasn't it? He hoped he didn't have to go through that again—the pleading, the bargaining…and then the eventual grief at not being able to stop Felicia from what she'd been so damned determined to do.

Yet, if Carly decided to have the baby, to keep it, she might want to take it on the road with her. And he'd hate that.

A baby needed regular hours, a loving home, a mom who was always there for it, a dad who—

Hey, now that was an idea. Maybe Carly would consider joint custody. Or maybe Ian could raise the baby himself.

He'd have to hire a housekeeper and a qualified nanny, though.

"What are you thinking?" Carly asked, drawing him from his thoughts and the plans he'd yet to think through.

The fact that his feelings, his choices, mattered to her eased his mind considerably and gave him… What? Hope?

"I'm actually okay with it," he said.

"I suspected you would be."

Then why wasn't her expression softening? Why wasn't she pleased by his support?

Hell, he'd marry her—if that would help, if it would make her feel better. And if he were to be honest with himself, he wouldn't mind having her live with him. He could see himself coming home to her each night, holding her in his arms, making love until they were both sated and smiling. But something told him she'd been so scarred by her parents' dysfunctional relationship and ultimate divorce that she would be opposed to the idea.

Of course, he could always try to convince her that some couples actually did make a go of it, that they could be happy together for fifty years or more. Take his grandparents, for example.

Yet maybe Ian had been scarred, too. His unhealthy relationship with Felicia had made him leery of trusting a woman to love him more than she loved her career. So now probably wasn't the time to make any serious decisions.

"Why don't we sleep on it?" he said.

Her brow arched as if he'd suggested they do so together—and in the same bed. He wouldn't be opposed to that. In fact, he'd like it. But that would take some courting, too—no matter how sexually compatible they'd been.

He told himself to exercise caution. After all, he had let his hormones convince him that he'd loved Felicia when they'd been in lust. Their relationship had ended badly, and he wasn't about to make that same mistake twice, especially when he and Carly had even more chemistry.

"We both have a lot to think about before we make any decisions," he added. "But I'm glad you told me."

"I figured you'd say that."

He wanted to add that he'd support her decision—no matter what it was—but that wasn't true. He wanted their baby. And he'd do whatever he could to be a big part of its life, even if he had to hire an attorney and fight Carly every step of the way.

Ian had taken the news well, Carly decided, although he'd remained quiet and introspective during dinner. He'd offered to help her with the dishes, but she'd sent him on his way, saying she needed time to think and would rather talk more in the morning.

He'd seemed relieved to have some time alone, too. He might have said that he was okay with the news, but it still must have taken him aback. Heck, she was okay with it, too, but that didn't mean the diagnosis hadn't thrown her for a loop.

After moving numbly through the kitchen, washing the dishes, putting the leftovers in the fridge and wiping down the countertops, Carly retreated to the guest room, where she'd left her purse and the paperwork the doctor's nurse had given her about pregnancy and what she could expect. She planned to look it over tonight.

But as she approached the doorway to her great-grandmother's bedroom, her steps slowed to a stop. She suddenly missed Granny more than ever and took a moment to walk inside, to surround herself with loving, comforting memories.

There was still a familiar hint of lavender lingering in the bedding, as well as in the Irish lace curtains. Other than the kitchen, it was the one place in the house in which Carly felt her great-grandmother's presence. But then again, maybe that had something to do with the dear old woman's portrait, which hung on the wall.

Camilla Cruz had painted it and captured something special in her expression—a knowing look that had put a twinkle in her eye, a warm smile. There was even the appearance of wisdom on her brow. She almost looked alive and ready to listen to Carly's hopes, joys and sorrows.

"Granny, I miss you so. And I wish you were really here." Carly took a seat in the antique rocker that rested near the bed, a hand-crocheted afghan draped over the wooden spindles in the back. She placed her hands on the slight swell of her stomach, where her baby grew, and looked at the portrait. "I'm pregnant. Imagine that."

She'd known about it for more than twenty-four hours now, yet it still seemed so surreal. The baby was real, though, and already its own person, yet Carly hadn't even been 100 percent sure of its existence until this afternoon.

As she set the rocker in motion, she envisioned holding her little one, rocking it. Singing lullabies.

She wasn't sure if it was a boy or girl, but that really didn't matter. Still, she wasn't sure how a baby would fit into her dream of performing. She'd planned to pursue her career for ten years or so, then retire and adopt children, creating a family of her own. Yet now, the timing had gone wrong, and her dreams had crisscrossed.

Did she care?

No, she already loved the life that grew inside of her. She'd just have to hire a nanny and take them both on tour. Somehow, she'd make it work. She just hoped Ian didn't make a fuss. For being an easygoing cowboy, he could sure get stubborn at times.

She just hoped this wasn't one of them.

Chapter Six

The next morning, Ian left Cheyenne outside with one of the teenage hands who'd come to help out. Then he let himself into the ranch house through the back door, put on a pot of coffee and waited in the kitchen for Carly to wake up.

Last night, after eating dinner with her and then returning to his place, he'd called Todd Adams, a cowhand who'd been looking for work, and asked him to help out on the Leaning R. Carly's brother Jason hadn't authorized him to do any hiring, but Ian planned to buy the ranch himself as soon as it went on the market, so he would pay the man out of his own pocket.

He'd already lined up Todd for the day, so he was free to talk to Carly. He had no idea how long he'd have to wait, but he was determined to talk to her first thing.

Carly didn't usually get up before nine, so he figured he'd just keep himself busy doing one of several fix-it projects Jason's new wife had told him about. One of those was to check out a leaky valve under the sink.

Ian was just getting started on that when Carly entered the kitchen wearing a pair of white shorts and an oversize green T-shirt. Her feet were bare, and her hair was damp. She'd taken a morning shower, but she hadn't put on any makeup. She didn't need to fuss with any of that, though. Anytime of the day or night, she was just about the prettiest woman he'd ever met.

She paused in the doorway and blinked when she spotted him kneeling near the open cupboard below the sink, a wrench in hand. Apparently she was surprised that he'd let himself in, something he'd done often when they'd been lovers.

"Good morning," he said, as if it were the most natural thing in the world for him to greet her like this. "I'm going to fix a leak under the sink before it gets any worse."

Her brow furrowed, and she cocked her head slightly, as if not buying his explanation.

He pointed toward the electric percolator on the counter. "Want some coffee? It's fresh."

"No, thanks. I'm…avoiding caffeine."

"Then how about a glass of milk?" He didn't mention that it would be good for the baby, but she must have known what he was getting at.

"No, I've never been a big milk drinker. But I'll have some in my cereal."

She crossed her arms and shifted her weight to one

hip. "You could have fixed the leak yesterday—or the day before. What's going on, Ian?"

He set down the wrench, then stood and tucked his thumbs into his front pockets. "I slept on it, Carly. Did you?"

She unwrapped her arms and made her way into the kitchen. "Well, I *did* go to sleep. But I'm still not sure what I'm going to do. I'd like to keep this between us right now."

There went the phone call to his grandparents, but he couldn't very well make an announcement like that until he could tell them what his plans were—like an upcoming marriage, raising a child on his own or even the possibility that he was heading into a custody battle, although he hoped it wouldn't come to that.

"I won't say anything," he said. "I take it you don't want to tell your brothers."

"No, not yet." She glanced at the far wall, where a couple of cardboard boxes were stacked. "For the time being, I have work to do. After breakfast, I plan to take up where Juliana left off on the inventory. I hope to have it done by the time she and Jason get back from Mexico."

"But it's almost finished." He hoped she wasn't planning to pack up the bedroom and the kitchen, then skedaddle. "You shouldn't pack up the rooms you'll be living out of."

"I won't do that, but the basement is full of stuff. And the attic is, too."

"I'll help you," he said.

Her lips parted, and her brow crinkled. "That's not necessary."

He pulled his hands from his pockets. "You shouldn't be doing any heavy lifting. So I'll do it for you. Just let me know where you want to start."

"Seriously?" She waited a beat before adding, "Who's going to work on the ranch? You haven't had enough help as it is."

"Actually, I just hired a new hand who's experienced and knows what to do before I even point it out."

She didn't ask whether he'd gotten permission from her brother, which was just as well. Ian didn't want her thinking he'd done anything out of line, but the last time he talked to Jason about the sale of the ranch, Jason gave him every reason to believe that both Carly and Braden were close to agreeing to list it. If Carly was planning to help with the inventory, then she'd obviously made up her mind.

"I'm not so sure about this." She paused, then bit down on her lower lip. "I mean, working in close quarters and all."

So it wasn't his offer to help with the heavy work that bothered her. She was worried about being tempted by him.

A slow smile spread across his lips. "Aw. I get it. But I wasn't trying to take advantage of you."

She seemed to shake it off—her attraction or whatever had her perplexed. "I'm not worried about that."

When she bit down on her bottom lip, he realized she wasn't being entirely truthful. She might be more concerned about fighting off her own desire.

"Oh, what the heck," she said, brightening. "I'll accept your offer to help. Besides, I really didn't feel like lugging around those boxes anyway, even though it has to be done."

If they were going to sell the ranch, it did. Although Ian wouldn't mind buying some of the stuff they didn't plan to keep. He was going to need furniture, dishes and other odds and ends. And since the ranch house had always felt cozy and welcoming to him, he wouldn't mind buying it furnished.

Carly crossed the kitchen, opened the pantry and pulled out a box of cereal. He watched her fill her bowl, then add milk and sugar. When she finished, she turned to him. "Want some?"

"I already ate. Back at my place."

She nodded, then took a seat at the table. For some reason, he felt as though he'd made a major stride today. She was going to let him help her inventory the rest of the house. Maybe they could reach other compromises along the way, and he wouldn't have to take her to court after all.

Still, they had a long way to go before they could coparent—or whatever they decided to call their new relationship.

If Ian thought that helping Carly pack and stack boxes would make her job any easier, he was wrong.

Well, physically speaking, she was glad to have him handle the heavy stuff, but the job of inventorying Granny's belongings was beginning to take a toll on her emotionally.

She doubted he knew it, though. Not based on the way he kept whistling.

What was the name of that song anyway? She didn't recognize it, but she liked the snappy tune.

Apparently, he was in a good mood, although she wasn't sure why. Maybe he was just glad to be indoors instead of outside, although she suspected he might be happy about being a daddy. That was a good sign, wasn't it? He could have been upset by the news, which would only make things more difficult for her.

"Are you okay?" he asked. "Is the dust getting to you? Your eyes are watery."

Carly swiped at her tears. "Being surrounded by all these things, by the memories, is making me a little weepy."

"I'm sorry."

"Don't be." She pushed aside the doll buggy Granny had given her, which had been one of her favorite playthings.

"Did that little stroller make you feel sentimental?" he asked.

She gave a little shrug. "On my sixth birthday, both of my parents were out of town and completely forgot what day it was. So Granny took me into town, purchased that little buggy, a new doll and several other gifts she let me pick out for myself. Afterward, we went to Caroline's Diner for a slice of German chocolate cake and a bowl of vanilla ice cream."

"Sounds like Granny did her best to make it up to you."

"She used to pick up the slack and do things like that

all the time, but I hadn't realized what she was doing when I was a kid." Carly sniffled, then smiled. "Do you know what else she did that day? She had everyone in the restaurant sing 'Happy Birthday' to me."

Ian eased close and slipped his arm around her in a gesture meant to be comforting. But as his alluring scent, a manly mixture of soap and musk, enveloped her, her thoughts turned to more recent memories, more recent emotions.

In spite of her resolve to keep her distance from the handsome cowboy, she leaned into him. "I'll be okay. Really."

She sniffed again, then turned away from him. But if she thought she could escape the warmth of his touch, it didn't work out that way. His scent seemed to cling to her as she returned to her work, tempting her, taunting her.

"What are you going to do with the toys?" he asked.

She had no idea. She could save them for her baby—*their* baby—but since she was between homes as well as jobs, she had no place to store them. "I suppose we should donate them to charity."

"All right. I'll stack them with the other things you plan to give away."

Carly scanned the basement, spotting the old Singer sewing machine, a vintage treadle model that had belonged to Granny's mother-in-law as well as an antique settee covered with a sheet. Next to it was a card table stacked with books and a slew of odds and ends.

It was going to take a long time to go through all of this and inventory it. She glanced at the old Saratoga trunk in the corner and blew out a heavy sigh. "What do you suppose is in there?"

"That's anyone's guess," Ian said. "Want me to open it?"

"Sure."

The old hinges creaked as he lifted the trunk's lid. "Looks like quilts." He pulled out the one on top, a colorful patchwork design.

Carly eased closer to get a better look at the handmade blanket. "It's beautiful. Look at all that intricate stitching. I wonder who made it."

"Granny, maybe." He continued to pull out several more, some of them stitched, but whose edges weren't finished. "I'm beginning to think these weren't hers. She never liked leaving things undone."

"She was also a better cook than a seamstress," Carly added. "Not that she couldn't hem a dress or darn socks. But she never used to sit around and sew for a hobby."

"There's something else in here." Ian handed a small cedar box to Carly.

As she accepted it, their hands brushed, and the warmth of his touch, as brief as it was, set off a spark that nearly singed her skin and sent her pulse rate into overdrive. She almost lost her grip on the box and dropped it, but she scrambled to gather her wits and her senses.

Still, her heart continued to pound as she peered inside the velvet-lined interior and spotted a man's ring, a filigreed cross on a silver chain and a gold pocket watch.

"Who do you think they belonged to?" Ian asked. It was a simple question, but his soft Southern twang did wacky things to her ability to think.

Her response came out in a near whisper as she set the box aside. "I have no idea."

The musty basement smelled of dust, but it was the scent of soap, leather and cowboy that stirred her hormones and her memories.

As her resolve weakened, she realized she would have to escape before she did something stupid—like fall into his arms.

Ian was sweet. And as sexy as sin. He was also charming when he put his mind to wooing her.

Of course, her father had been a charmer, too.

Not that Ian was anything like her dad. But still. She had to keep her wits about her until she could decide whether he was just being a thoughtful expectant father or trying to make her see things his way.

As she turned her back to him, a small puff of brown fur scurried across the top of her sandaled foot, and she let out a scream as though a cougar had just entered the basement. Without a conscious thought, she spun back to Ian and nearly climbed up his body. "Get it out of here!"

He laughed, but he scooped her into his arms, rescuing her from the tiny critter. "He's more afraid of you than you are of him."

"I don't care. Mice and rats give me the willies."

And clinging to Ian was giving her pause. But she couldn't fall back into a sexual relationship with him. So, with her cheeks glazing hot and her heart soaring, she unwrapped herself from his arms. "Will you please shoo that mouse outside? I'm going to call it a day."

"He's long gone by now—probably suffering from a cardiac arrest."

"Good," she said, as she hurried up the stairs to the main part of the house.

"We can always get a cat," he called out behind her. "That ought to keep the mice and rats at bay."

Maybe so. But who was going to keep Ian and temptation at bay?

As the days passed, the slight bulge in Carly's tummy seemed to practically double in size, and she soon found that a lot of her pants felt tight. So she took a break after inventorying the basement and before tarting on the attic and drove into town to find some looser clothing to wear.

She wasn't big enough to warrant a purchase at the maternity shop in Wexler, but she suspected she could find something to tide her over a month or two at the Mercantile in downtown Brighton Valley. And she'd been right.

After buying a couple pairs of pants and several tops that would work, she returned to her pickup. Well, almost.

A walk past Caroline's Diner triggered a craving for lemon meringue pie.

How about that? Once Carly had learned that she was pregnant, all the signs and symptoms had flared up, making the diagnosis real. Of course, she'd always craved something sweet to eat whenever she strolled past the diner.

For some reason, the local eatery, with its yellow walls, white café-style curtains and cozy booths, offered her comfort and a feeling of coming home—almost as much as the Leaning R did. Or rather, like it had when Granny had been there.

She'd no more than walked inside when she spotted the blackboard that advertised the daily special for $8.99. In yellow chalk, someone had written "What the Sheriff Ate," followed by "Fried Chicken, Mashed Potatoes and Gravy, Buttered Carrots and Cherry Pie à la mode."

As Carly turned to the refrigerated case that displayed yummy desserts, she spotted Stu Jeffries, the new mayor, sitting at the counter. When he recognized Carly, he pushed his plate aside, picked up his bill and got up from his seat.

Mayor Jeffries, a short, stout businessman in his mid to late fifties, snatched his Stetson from the chair next to where he'd been sitting and plopped it on his head, reminding Carly of a giant thumb tack.

"Why, Carly Rayburn! You're just the person I want to talk to."

She greeted him with a smile. "Hi, Stu. What's up?"

"First of all, I'd like to compliment you. Marcia and I were at the Stagecoach Inn last Friday night when you and the Leaning R foreman played. I'd meant to talk to you afterward, but you slipped out before I got a chance."

Carly had noticed that the mayor and his wife had

occupied one of the corner booths. But she wasn't about to tell him why she'd hightailed it out of the honky-tonk so quickly. "What can I do for you?"

"First of all, I wanted you to know how much we enjoyed that duet. You and Ian—that's his name, right?"

She nodded.

"Anyway, the two of you are very talented. A real hit. Marcia told me to ask you to perform at the Founder's Day Festival in a couple of weeks—and again at the dance that evening at the Grange Hall. How about it?"

Carly's heart leaped at the praise as well as the invitation. But when she imagined what Ian's reaction would be, her pulse hit a snag.

"We're charging admission at the dance," the smiling mayor added. "And the proceeds are going toward the new program for disabled children at the Brighton Valley Kids Club."

She hadn't known about the new program, but she certainly could support something like that. And while Ian had made it clear he'd never go on stage with her again, she wondered if he'd change his mind because it was for such a good cause.

It was hard to say, but if he still wouldn't budge, she couldn't let that screw up her own opportunity. So she went out on a limb and said, "I'd be delighted to perform that day. And I'm sure Ian will, too."

"I'm glad to hear that. Our PR committee has been working hard on this, so we'll get you on the schedule as soon as we can. And it just so happens that Jolene, one of the clerks down at City Hall, plans to drop it off at the print shop this afternoon—right before her softball game with the Hot Mamas League. So if I hurry back to the office, I should be able to add you to that brochure, too."

Carly wasn't sure what Ian would say when he realized she'd already made a commitment for them. But at least the proceeds of the evening dance were going to help disabled children. So how could he object?

Besides, she had two weeks to talk him into it. And a whole recipe box of tempting goodies to soften the blow.

Ian was at the ranch house painting the front porch railing when Carly drove up. Cheyenne, who'd kept getting in his way all morning—bless her ever-lovin' puppy heart—trotted toward the small pickup, the stump of her little tail wagging. She was no doubt hoping to find a more enthusiastic playmate than he'd been for the past hour.

Carly opened the driver's door, slid out of the truck, then stooped to pat the rascally pup. "Hey! What are you doing, girl?"

Cheyenne was so excited to get an ear rub that her little tail wagged her entire hind end from side to side.

"Uh-oh," Carly said. "You have white paint on your fur."

Ian laughed. "I'm not surprised. She wasn't content to nap or just watch."

Carly reached into the cab and withdrew a couple of shopping bags that bore the Mercantile branding.

"Did you find any bargains?" he asked.

"Not really. But I picked up some pants and blouses that I can wear for a while."

He glanced at her waistline, which seemed to have expanded since her arrival. Apparently, their baby was growing, which pleased him. But he figured he'd better bite back a proud-papa smile.

"What are you doing?" she asked as she approached the house.

"The railing was loose, so I fixed it. And now I'm giving it a coat of paint."

She nodded, then bit down on her bottom lip—a habit she had when she was pensive or stressed.

Ian didn't like seeing her troubled, so he set the paintbrush across the lid of the can and got to his feet. "What's wrong?"

"Nothing." She brightened momentarily, then went back to biting her lip. "I…uh…ran into Mayor Jeffries in town."

Ian lifted his arm, wiped the perspiration from his brow with his shirtsleeve and grinned. "You mean to tell me the new mayor shops at the only ladies' dress shop in town?"

She chuckled at his attempt to lighten her mood. "No, that's not where I saw him. He was at the diner."

Since Carly didn't usually find it newsworthy to tell him about the various people she ran into while in town, he waited for her to continue.

"You might not have noticed, but Stu and his wife were at the Stagecoach Inn last Friday night and saw our performance."

Again, Ian remained silent. He suspected that she

had something she was worried about telling him. And that she didn't expect him to be happy about it. If that was the case, he wasn't going to make it any easier for her to announce whatever it was. So he crossed his arms and stood tall.

"He'd like for us to perform at the Founder's Day Festival, which will be held in Town Square in two weeks. Then, that evening, we'd play at the community dance at the Grange Hall." Carly glanced down at her boots, then back to Ian and smiled, her blue eyes damn near sparkling. "I hope you don't mind, but it's for a really good cause—the new program at the Brighton Valley Kids Club for disabled children. So I told him we'd do it."

Ian stiffened. "You agreed for both of us?"

Tears welled in her eyes, and she swiped at them. "What's one more little singing gig? It's not like I'm trying to drag you to the Grand Ole Opry. It's just a small-town thing. Besides, all the money they make at the dance will go to a good cause. Surely you can't say no to that."

"You know good and well how I feel about performing."

Her eyes flooded with more emotion, and she sniffled, then wiped the moisture away again. "Damn these hormones."

Ian hated to see her cry, but he wasn't about to admit it. And he couldn't give in to her like her father had always done. The last thing he needed was for her to think she had him wrapped around her pinkie, too. "I'm not going to do it, Carly."

"Not even for those poor little kids?"

Sure, he'd do just about anything to benefit children in need. But Carly was working him, and he had to hold his ground. "If I thought you were only concerned about charity, that'd be one thing. But I know what you're really trying to do. You want me to eventually agree to go on the road with you, and I'm not going to do it."

She blew out an exasperated sigh. "You frustrate the heck out of me, Ian. And yes, I'll admit that I want to perform in the future—with you, if possible. But you don't seem to care about what's important to me. I need to make a name for myself, even if Brighton Valley is only a stepping stone."

"You're a *Rayburn*, Carly. You already have a name for yourself."

"That's *not* what I meant." She crossed her arms, the tears a thing of the past now as she dug in her boots for battle. "At first, I wanted you to perform with me because you're so talented. And also because we have good chemistry—and not *just* in bed. But now it's a matter of principle. We need to be able to work together and do what's right."

Ian clucked his tongue and shook his head. She was taking this way out of context. "Granted, it's a good cause. And I'd be happy to write a generous check to the charity itself. So don't lecture me about doing what's right."

"You don't get it, Ian. If we can't learn to compromise and respect each other's ideals and honor our dreams, how will we ever be able to coparent?"

Her last blow hit below the belt. There was nothing he'd like more in the world than parenting their child with her—even before the birth. He wanted to argue, to object, to flat-out refuse. But she'd argued him into a corner and there was no other way out than to agree.

"Okay, Carly. I'm not happy about this, but I'll do it—just this one last time."

Her anger melted into a breezy smile. "Thank you, Ian. You won't be sorry. I promise."

He wasn't sorry about performing, but he was already regretting the fact that she'd managed to talk him into doing something he'd been dead set against. Again.

But on the upside, if he could convince her to be happy performing in two-bit venues here in Brighton Valley, then maybe that would be enough for her and she'd agree to stick close to home, where they could actually create a family of their own.

Then maybe they could learn to parent their baby together. And Ian could be the husband and father he'd always wanted to be.

Chapter Seven

Ian steered clear of Carly for the next couple of days—at least, that's what he seemed to be doing. At first, she'd made up her mind to leave him alone until his mood improved. But it soon became apparent that he was avoiding her and she would have to make the first move.

While she hadn't meant to make him angry, she should have realized that a man like Ian didn't like being pressed to do something he didn't want to do.

And Carly had pushed him too hard. She not only owed him an apology, but she ought to do something to mend fences.

The only plan she could come up with was to tell him how sorry she was over a home-cooked meal made entirely from Granny's recipes.

So the next morning, after Ian and the ranch hands had ridden out together, she came up with the perfect menu and made a list of all the ingredients she needed to purchase at the market. Next, she slipped a note under Ian's cabin door, telling him she needed to talk to him and inviting him to dinner this evening.

When she returned home from her shopping trip, she took a shower, then shampooed and styled her hair. After slipping on a new pair of black stretch pants and an oversize mint-colored blouse, she stood in front of the bathroom mirror and primped a bit longer than she'd intended. After all, she and Ian weren't lovers anymore.

But they would be parents. So, for that reason, it was best for everyone involved if she put her best foot forward, apologized and did whatever she could to put them back on even ground.

Satisfied with her appearance and her game plan, she headed for the kitchen and made a meal sure to soften his heart.

While the meat loaf was in the oven, she set the table with Granny's best dishes, which she'd found packed in one of the stacked boxes in the dining room. She'd wanted everything to be perfect tonight, so while she was at the market, she'd also picked up some candles as well as a bouquet of flowers, which would add a nice touch.

A knock sounded at the front door, taking her by surprise. Ever since they'd first made love, Ian had let himself into the house through the mudroom. Obviously, things were different between them now, although she was determined to shake the awkwardness—as well as the mounting sexual tension that threatened to unravel her whenever he was near.

Still, she was ready for his arrival.

Or so she thought.

As she swung open the door and spotted the handsome cowboy on the porch, her heart took a tumble. He wore a Western shirt—a soft blue plaid she'd never seen before—and black jeans. He removed his hat, revealing damp hair—fresh from the shower.

"Am I too early?" he asked.

"No, you're right on time. Come on in." She stepped aside and waited for him to enter.

Instead, he glanced over his shoulder and called out, "Cheyenne, come on or I'll leave you outside."

Moments later, the black-and-white pup bounded up the steps wearing a red bandanna around her neck. Apparently, Carly and Ian weren't the only ones who'd spiffed up for their dinner.

"Aren't you cute," Carly said as she stooped to pat the puppy.

Ian continued to stand on the porch, his hat in hand. "So what's on your mind?"

"First of all," she said, stepping aside so Ian and Cheyenne could enter, "I want to apologize. I never should have agreed to perform as a duo when you'd made it clear how you felt about going on stage. It's just that I was so excited about being asked, that I said yes without a thought. But I was wrong, and I'm sorry. It won't happen again."

When he didn't say anything, she wondered if he

was going to accept her apology. But then, he'd come to dinner, hadn't he?

"To make matters worse," she added, "I pushed you until you agreed to sing with me, which wasn't fair. Will you forgive me?"

A slow smile spread across his face. "You promised not to agree to any more singing engagements on my behalf. But what about pushing me?"

She returned his grin. "I can try, but I don't want to make promises I might not be able to keep."

"That's what I figured." He placed his hat on the rack near the door. "You didn't need to invite me to dinner, though. Besides, I already agreed to perform with you."

She straightened. "I know, but this seemed like the best way to let you know I'm sincere. And while I admit that I'm glad you agreed, I'll respect your feelings about singing in public next time."

"I'd appreciate that." He took a whiff and broke into a broad smile. "I sure like the smell of your apologies. What's on the menu tonight?"

She grinned. "Granny's famous meat loaf, roasted red potatoes and buttered green beans with slivered almonds. I hope you'll like it."

"No doubt about that."

As Carly led Ian through the living room and into the kitchen, he said, "You sure went all out. You're even using Granny's good dishes."

"Like I said, I want to do this right."

Minutes later, they were seated at the table, enjoying a meal that Ian said was a good as any Granny had ever made. Carly was thrilled with the compliment.

"I know you don't want to hear this," Ian said, "but you belong on the Leaning R."

His words rang true. Granny had said the same thing to her, and at the time, she'd been right. But Carly had outgrown small-town life. And she wanted her child to have more opportunities than could be found on a ranch.

She took a sip of water from her goblet. "Maybe I did belong here once—when I was a kid. But not anymore."

"I'm not talking about a permanent residence here, but you're a part of this ranch, Carly. As much as or more than your great-grandmother was. And in case you haven't figured it out, this is the place you always come home to."

Carly wasn't so sure about being a part of the ranch. It did feel like home, but it should. Her best times had been spent on the Leaning R with Granny. "I have a lot of good memories here, but this isn't where my future lies."

"I understand that." He speared the last potato on his plate and put it in his mouth. Moments later, he added, "I take it that you've let Jason know you've agreed to the sale."

She nodded. "Yes, I have. And truthfully, I'll be sorry to see it go—especially to strangers. But it's not feasible for us to keep it in the family."

His lips parted as if he was going to say something—or maybe disagree—but he kept quiet.

"So what about you?" she asked. "Don't you have a place you call home?"

"I did, but my granddad sold it a few years back. And even though he and my grandma moved to Florida and are living in a condominium now, it still feels like home when I visit them."

"Really?" She found that hard to believe. "Why is that?"

"Because a home is more about the people who live there than the actual house itself."

She thought about that for a while. Granny had been more of a mother to her than the one who'd given her birth. And maybe that's why she always found herself returning to the Leaning R. Even now, after her great-grandmother's passing, it was still the only place where Granny seemed to be. At least the memories of her were here.

"You mentioned growing up on your granddad's ranch," Carly said. "What about your parents? Where did they live?"

"I don't remember my mom. She died in a car accident when I was three."

Carly had never really talked to him about his past because it hadn't seemed to matter. But for some reason, it mattered now.

"I'm sorry," she said. "What about your dad?"

Ian studied his empty plate for the longest time, and for a while, she wondered if he was even going to answer the question.

"When I was three, my parents left me with my grandparents while they took off to celebrate their anniversary in town. Apparently, they got into a heated argument, which led to the crash. At least, that's what it said in the police report. My father was sent to prison for vehicular manslaughter."

Carly had no idea what to say, especially when another "I'm sorry" seemed inadequate.

"While my dad was in jail, I lived with my grandparents at their cattle ranch near Dallas." Ian leaned back in his chair, his pose anything but relaxed. "When he was finally paroled, I moved to Fort Worth with him, but that didn't last very long."

She couldn't believe that they'd once been lovers, yet he'd never revealed anything about his early years. He seemed to know a lot about hers, though. Some she'd shared with him, and other things he might have learned from Granny.

But what about Ian? Not that she hadn't cared or been curious about his past before, but she'd been so convinced that they didn't have a future together that she'd once thought it wasn't any of her business. Yet now with the baby coming, learning more about him suddenly seemed important.

She leaned forward, her forearms resting on the table. "What do you mean? Why didn't you stay with your father?"

"He was an alcoholic, and whenever he went on a binge, he would miss work and get fired. Or he'd get in fights at bars or wherever. Each time he was arrested, I'd end up back at the ranch with my grandparents."

No wonder he was so close to them. "I'm sorry, Ian. I had no idea life was so difficult for you as a child."

"It wasn't so bad. At least, not at the ranch. I loved it there and learned how to rope and ride and work with cattle."

"So when they sold it, that's how you ended up here?"

He gave a simple shrug. "Actually, I was just passing through town and stopped at Caroline's Diner for lunch. I mentioned to Margie, the waitress, that I was a cowhand looking for work, and she introduced me to Granny, who was having a piece of peanut butter pie with a friend."

"Margie's a real sweetheart," Carly said, "but she has a way of asking questions and passing news along."

Ian laughed. "Yeah, I learned that quickly. But she did me a favor that day. Otherwise, I wouldn't have landed a job at the Leaning R. It was a win-win for Granny and me."

"In what way?" Carly asked.

"She needed a son as badly as I needed a family, so we looked after each other."

Carly was touched by his affection for her great-grandma, yet something niggled at her. "Why did you stick around, even after she passed away? I mean, I know my dad wasn't the easiest guy to work for."

"You're right about that." Ian took a chug of his iced tea. "No offense, Carly, but Charles Rayburn didn't give a rip about ranching."

Ian had that right. Her father had been put in charge of Granny's estate for a year before she died, but he was too caught up in his own company and his own life to even visit. But then, he hadn't ever had time for Carly, either. Why would it be any different for the woman who'd practically raised him?

"I guess you could say that I'm still looking out for Granny's best interests," Ian added.

Carly hadn't expected him to say that—or to stick around after Granny had died. Apparently Ian wasn't the tumbleweed she'd imagined him to be.

What else about him had she misread? It was going to take more than one intimate dinner for her to find out, she supposed.

"I appreciate all you've done around here," she told him. "And the fact that you're helping us sell a place you've considered a home."

Ian studied her for a moment. A long moment.

Again, she thought he might be pondering a comment, but if he had something to say, he kept it to himself.

Finally, he spoke. "Believe it or not, I'm happier than I've been in a long time. And that's why I plan to settle down in Brighton Valley for good."

He'd made that clear early on, so she wasn't surprised. But that was also the reason they'd never be happy together, at least not in the long run. Their dreams for the future were as different as their pasts.

Carly placed a hand on her baby bump, caressing it and wondering about the little one who grew there—and if he or she would inherit traits from both Ian and Carly.

Raising a baby together wasn't going to be easy. She just hoped they would be able to put aside their differences in order to become a better mom and dad than the ones who'd birthed them.

* * *

Ian pushed back his chair, got up from the kitchen table and began to gather the dishes.

"Don't worry about cleaning up," Carly said. "I'll do it after you go."

"I don't mind helping. Besides, this is my way of showing my appreciation for dinner." Ian carried the stack of dishes to the counter. After reaching for the plastic bottle of soap from the cupboard under the sink, he turned on the hot water. "That was the best meal I've had in a long time."

"It was no big deal," Carly said. "I had fun cooking tonight."

He didn't doubt that for a minute. Carly was far more domestic than she realized. She also had a way of doing special little things for him—at least, she had when they'd been sleeping together.

One day, she'd picked wildflowers on her walk in the meadow. She'd brought them into his cabin and put them in water in the only vase she could find—a mason jar. Then she set them on the dinette table, brightening up his home as well as his day.

Another time, she'd purchased a cookie jar for him in town and filled it with candy because she knew he had a sweet tooth.

Was it any wonder he believed she had a domestic streak?

She'd insisted that she didn't, though. And he suspected that was because she feared acknowledging it would encourage him—or maybe it would hamper her dream of becoming a star.

"Oh, no! Cheyenne, give me that! Look what you've done."

Ian turned to see his rascally pup with Carly's black dress shoe in her mouth. She'd done a real number on the black spiked heel, chomping at it until she'd left little bite marks up and down. "I'm sorry, Carly. I owe you a shopping trip and a new pair of heels."

Carly, who now held the sexy shoe in her hand, slowly shook her head. "Don't worry about it. Something tells me I won't be wearing these for a while anyway."

She appeared to be resigned to the puppy's mischief as well as the change in her immediate plans for the future.

Did that mean she intended to have the baby and not give it up—or worse? He sure hoped so. He didn't want to lose another child before he had the opportunity to hold it, to love it. To protect it.

Ian shut off the water, dried his hands and crossed the room to where Cheyenne sat, perplexed that she'd lost her newfound toy. "I brought you to dinner, thinking that you'd remember your manners and stick close to me. You're not supposed to roam the house, looking for trouble."

"She was just being a puppy," Carly said. "I'll have to pick up some of those rawhide strips for her to chew on next time she comes to visit."

So there would be a next time. He was glad to hear it.

His life had taken a nice turn when he'd stopped in Brighton Valley that day and met Granny. Then it had really looked up when he'd met Carly. But as amazing as their short-lived time together had been, Carly only had eyes for the fame and glory Ian had left behind.

And he wasn't sure where that would leave him and their child.

Carly and Ian arrived early at the Founder's Day Festival with Ian in the driver's seat of his truck and his guitar resting between them. He lucked out when a car in front of Caroline's Diner pulled out of a space, allowing him to park along the tree-shaded main drag of Brighton Valley.

"I really appreciate this," Carly said again as she slid out the passenger door.

"I know. You've mentioned that a time or two." He reached for his guitar, then locked the truck.

They seemed to have reached a truce and an understanding, which was good.

As they headed toward Town Square, Carly nudged him with her elbow. "Can I ask you something?"

"Sure." He stole a glance at her, then continued to set his sights on the route ahead.

"What are you afraid of?"

He shot her a second glance, this one sharp and pointed. "What are you talking about?"

"I mean, I respect your wishes and all, and I'll keep my promise to let you be. But what's your real reason for not wanting to perform in front of an audience? You certainly don't seem to be the least bit nervous."

Nervous? No. But he was worried. Worried about being found out. He liked his peaceful existence and didn't want to jeopardize it by having anyone—especially Felicia—find out who he was, where he was and what he was doing.

As the soles of their boots crunched along the dusty sidewalk, he said, "Maybe I'm just afraid you'll try to drag me out on tour, and I'm happy here in Brighton Valley with the quiet life I've chosen."

If he did tell Carly who he really was, would she be content to let it go? Or would she hang on to his identity like a hungry Rottweiler with a meaty bone?

Even though she thought he was just a simple cowboy, she'd nearly pestered him to death.

He supposed he'd have to tell her—one of these days. But now didn't seem to be the time. If he knew Carly, she'd use her mother's contacts to look up Felicia, who hadn't had a platinum hit since Ian had written his last song for her.

"I don't really understand your refusal," Carly added, "but like I said, I'll respect it."

"Thanks."

They continued several blocks until they reached Town Square, with its park-like grounds and big clock tower in the center of the lawn.

The townsfolk who'd already gathered to wait for the festivities to start stood in intimate clusters or sat at the various rented tables and chairs that had been set up in the shade.

Near the courthouse, The Barbecue Pit, a local restaurant that catered parties and special events, had already brought in their old-style chuck wagon with its portable grill, setting off the aroma of wood smoke and sizzling beef, pork and chicken. The cooks, in their black cowboy hats and white aprons, turned the meat and brushed a spicy sauce over the top.

A stage had been set up, and several bands had begun to gather already.

"What time are we supposed to perform?" Ian asked Carly.

"I'm not sure, but there's the mayor." She pointed to Stu Jeffries, who was talking to Arthur Bellows, one of the town councilmen.

The mayor, who was dressed in his finest Western wear, looked especially short and squat next to the tall, slender councilman. But he seemed to puff up a wee bit taller when he spotted Ian and Carly approaching him.

"Excuse me," Stu told Arthur. Then he turned to welcome Carly with a broad smile and shake hands with Ian.

"You have no idea how happy I'll be to introduce you two when you get on stage today," he said. "Your performance at the Stagecoach Inn rocked the house. How long have you been singing together?"

"Not long," Ian said.

The mayor hooked his thumbs into the front pockets of his spankin' new jeans. "Well, kids, I'm here to tell you that the two of you are going to go far. My wife and I think you have what it takes to be stars."

Carly nudged Ian with her elbow. "What did I tell you?"

He arched a brow, reminding her of their agreement.

Whether Stu knew it or not, this performance, and the dance later at the Grange Hall, was their last hurrah. After tonight, Ian would go back to his life on the Leaning R.

"Did you see the posters we put up around the county?" Stu asked.

Ian stiffened. "What posters?"

"Advertisements for today's event." The short mayor seemed to rise up an inch or two taller. "My wife, Marcia, took a photo of you two when you were playing at the Stagecoach Inn the other night. You looked so natural together, and the shot we had was so clear, we used it to promote the dance tonight."

Ian flinched. His photo was being plastered all over the county?

He nearly took Carly aside and chewed her out for not telling him about the mayor's PR plan. But how clear could the picture be? The mayor and his wife had been seated in one of the booths, and the honky-tonk had been dark.

His initial concern eased and he began to relax. Besides, what were the chances that Felicia would see it—or get wind of it—and come looking for him?

Chapter Eight

Ian and Carly's performance in Town Square went without a hitch. And by the time they wrapped up with the love song Ian had written about him and Carly, the crowd went wild, giving them a standing ovation.

As they took a final bow, Ian didn't dare glance Carly's way. He knew what he'd see in her expression. She had to be walking on clouds at the obvious appreciation and community validation. But the two of them had made a deal, and he expected her to honor it.

As they stepped off the stage, several people in the crowd swarmed around them, praising them and asking where they would perform next.

"Do you guys play for parties?" one man asked. "My wife and I are celebrating our twenty-fifth wedding anniversary next month, and I'd like to hire you."

"No, I'm afraid this is a onetime thing." Ian sensed Carly's disappointment, but he wasn't about to give in to her again.

A buxom, big-haired brunette dressed in tight jeans and a red silky blouse pressed a business card into Ian's hand. "I'm Molly Carmichael with Star-Studded Nights Entertainment. If you two are looking for a manager, I'd like to talk to you. Maybe we can step over to one of those tables and have a little chat."

"I'd be interested in talking to you," Carly said. "But Ian isn't looking for a manager."

"That's a shame." The attractive brunette focused her baby blues on Ian. "Are you already represented?"

In a way, yes. Ian had worked with Samuel R. Layton, one of the top managers in the country. So if he wanted to get back to work, one simple phone call to Sam was all it would take to fill his schedule of appearances for the next year.

Ian lifted his Stetson and raked a hand through his hair. "Thanks for the offer, Ms. Carmichael, but I'm not planning to perform publicly anymore."

"Now that's an even bigger shame," she said.

He supposed that depended upon how you looked at it. He'd had his fill of the fame and glamour…as well as the phoniness of people wanting to ride his coattails in order to make a name for themselves. And that was one reason he hadn't come clean with Carly.

She merely thought of him as a cowboy or a rancher, and she'd pressed him hard enough as it was. What would she do if she knew of his past success on the stage?

He watched Carly take the woman's card, wanting to object, to ask, what about the baby? But he had no right to interfere in her life.

Ian did have paternal rights, though. And he'd exercise them if he needed to. Surely Carly didn't plan to go out on the road while she was pregnant.

In spite of his resolve not to insist that she do things his way, he slipped his arm around her expanding waist, staking a claim he had no right to make.

"When do we need to head over to the Grange Hall?" he asked her.

Apparently, his boldness didn't surprise her, because she seemed to lean into him. "Before dark, but the sooner the better."

"Then we ought to go." He turned his focus to their wannabe manager. "Will you excuse us, Ms. Carmichael?"

"Of course." The woman smiled at Carly. "I'll be in my office on Monday morning, so I'll expect your call."

"All right." Carly tucked the business card into her pocket.

"Come on." Ian guided Carly through the crowd and across the street. As they headed for his truck, he said, "Thanks for not pushing me to meet with that woman."

"We made a deal. Besides, I've come to realize that I can't change your mind when it's made up."

He was glad she'd finally come to that conclusion, but could he change *her* mind? He'd let the baby questions pile up ever since he'd first learned she was pregnant. She hadn't wanted to discuss the future when she was still trying to get a perspective on the present. But he couldn't help bringing it up now.

"How does the baby fit into your career plans?" he asked.

"I'll figure out something."

Like what? Hiring a nanny to take on the road with her? He'd known performers who'd done that, but it hadn't worked out very well in some cases.

"Don't forget," he said, "I want to be a part of our child's life, so you won't be raising it on your own."

"I appreciate that, Ian. And just for the record, I know you'll be a good daddy."

It wouldn't take much to be an improvement on her old man's parenting. Or his own father's, for that matter. But come hell or high water, Ian was bound and determined to do right by his son or daughter—or to die trying.

He felt a rising compulsion to tell Carly he'd make a good husband, too. But sharing his feelings for her— which were complicated, to say the least—wasn't as easy as talking to her about their child.

As they approached his truck, Carly gave his shirtsleeve a gentle tug. "Do you think the baby will inherit our musical talent?"

He smiled. "I imagine so. Maybe I should write a lullaby or something so we can encourage a love of music early on."

"That's sweet."

They continued on to where he'd left his pickup. When they arrived at the parking space, she asked, "Did your parents sing or play any instruments?"

"Not that I know of. But my grandma McAllister plays the organ at her church."

Carly seemed to ponder that as he opened the passenger door for her. After he got in and started the engine, she continued with her questions. "When did you learn to play the guitar?"

"My grandma insisted that I take piano lessons when I was seven, but once I laid hands on my first guitar, I was hooked. Before long, I was playing country music instead of old hymns."

"It's nice that she encouraged you. My mom always tried to talk me out of following in her footsteps."

Ian figured that's why she'd been so determined to make a name for herself. And while he believed she had talent and ambition, he wondered if at least a small part of that was rebellion.

"Actually," he said, "my grandma wasn't all that supportive of my switch to country music, so I taught myself to play the guitar."

"Now I'm really impressed."

As far as he was concerned, he hadn't had any other options. He'd been a quiet and introspective kid who'd often turned to his instrument for solace. And that was about the time he began writing tunes of his own.

"Did your grandmother forgive you for giving up gospel tunes?"

Ian couldn't help but chuckle. "Oh, yeah. She's a real sweetheart and would never hold anything against me—or anyone else. But we did strike a compromise. Whenever I'm in Sarasota, which is where she and my granddad retired, I play for her church's old gospel hour."

Carly turned in the seat, her eyes bright, her smile contagious. "That's very cool. So you really don't mind performing for an audience."

"I told you that was never an issue."

She studied him a moment, her smile waning ever so slightly. "You're an interesting man, Ian McAllister."

She didn't know the half of it.

Was now the time to tell her about his years of playing with Felicia?

The thought of confessing his past didn't last long. He'd finally convinced her that he didn't want to perform, and they seemed to be reestablishing a relationship—of one kind or another. So he bit his tongue and continued to drive to the Grange Hall. One more gig, and his performing days were over.

He just wished Carly would make that same decision—at least until their child was older. But when he glanced across the seat and saw the glimmer of anticipation in her pretty blue eyes, he had his doubts.

Carly and Ian were even better received at the Grange Hall than when they'd performed in Town Square. As he strummed the final chord of their last song, even the couples on the dance floor clapped and cheered. She felt a rush of elation she'd never expected. Still, she'd agreed this would be their final act together.

In fact, knowing how Ian had dug in his boot heels, she'd actually expected him to grab her hand and hightail it outside before the applause ended. But he surprised her stopping by the refreshment table and getting them each a glass of punch.

When Bud Mobley and his trio took the stage next and began to play a slow country love song, Ian reached for her hand. But instead of heading for the door, he led her onto the dance floor.

As he slipped his arms around her, he whispered in her ear, "Just for old times' sake."

For that very reason—and perhaps for another reason she didn't want to admit—she stepped into his familiar embrace. The musky scent of his woodsy aftershave snaked around her, holding her captive in its warmth and with the seductive sway of his body.

As they danced cheek to cheek, all the longing she'd ever felt for him rushed back full force, and she struggled to hold it in check.

Ian was an amazing lover, a good man—one of the finest she'd ever met. And she cared about him—far more than she'd ever let him know. More than she dared to even ponder, if she knew what was good for her.

Yet when Bud Mobley crooned on about a love that would never die and a man being the kind of lover a woman could build her dreams on, Carly almost believed it was possible.

Could she and Ian find a way to compromise about their future plans? Could they create a home in which to raise a family, while she pursued a singing career on her own?

He drew her near, his soft breath warm against her neck. She felt herself weakening. And for a moment, she wasn't nearly as eager to see her name in bright lights. Not that she'd given up the dream, but it just didn't feel so pressing.

She'd never thought that loving Ian and living in Brighton Valley for the rest of her life would be enough for her. But now, as she leaned into him, her heart swelling and desire building deep in her core, she wasn't so sure about that.

Did she dare give this up, give him up? Of course, that was assuming he wanted her. But if she'd ever had any doubts about his feelings for her, they eased when the song ended and he continued to hold her close.

She could have slipped out of his arms, but if truth be told, she'd missed his embrace.

And she'd missed *him*.

"Come on," he whispered against her ear. "Let's go home."

She couldn't have objected, even if she'd wanted to. She actually liked the sound of going home to the Leaning R with Ian, no matter how temporary that home might be.

The ride back to the ranch was quiet, yet the cab sparked with desire and pent-up emotion. She risked a glance at the handsome cowboy, at the intensity of his stare as he peered through the windshield at the road ahead. And she suspected he felt it, too.

Once they arrived home, they walked along the path that led to both the house and his cabin. A full moon glowed in the star-splattered sky overhead, making the evening seem almost magical. And even though Carly told herself to ignore it, to tell Ian good-night and go on her way, something much stronger overrode her common sense.

"Would you like to come in for a cup of coffee or tea?" she asked.

"Sure. That sounds good to me."

She led the way to the front porch, unlocked the door and let him inside. But once they entered the house, she didn't dart off to the kitchen. Instead, she turned to the man who'd fathered her baby and touched her heart.

Could she compromise her dream? Could she lay her hope on having a real home and family? A week or so ago, her answer to both questions would have been no. But now she wasn't so sure.

"I want to thank you again for performing with me tonight," she said.

"No problem. When I make a deal, I stick to it."

As their eyes met and their gazes locked, she eased closer to him. She might be sorry for this later, but she reached up, cupped his cheek with one hand, felt the light bristle of his beard.

He placed his palm over the top of her hand, holding her touch against his face, melding her to him as if they'd never been apart.

She didn't know why it was so difficult for her to speak, to tell him she'd like to make love with him again, but she couldn't find her voice. Still, her heart pounded in anticipation.

"I've missed you," he said. "And I've missed the closeness we once shared."

She'd missed him, too. She'd never known a man like Ian.

Without another word, she slipped her hand around to the back of his neck and drew his mouth to hers.

The moment Carly's lips touched his, Ian pulled her into his arms and kissed her with a longing he hadn't expected. He'd told himself it had been for the best when they'd split up, yet being around her again had him questioning that. Now more than ever.

As she leaned into him, he intensified the kiss, his tongue seeking hers, sweeping, dipping and tasting.

It had been so long since he'd felt this kind of fire, this urgency, and he couldn't seem to get enough of her.

As their bodies pressed together, their hands stroked, caressed, explored. When he sought her breast, his thumb skimmed across a taut nipple, and she whimpered. Making love with Carly had always been incredible, yet he'd almost forgotten just how good they were together. When she ended the kiss, he thought he might die if she told him she was having second thoughts. But she remained in his arms.

"I'm willing to take this to the bedroom," she said, "if you are."

"There's nothing I'd like more."

Carly led him to the guest room in which they'd made love in the past. She'd once laughed about it, telling him she didn't feel right about sleeping with him in Granny's bed, especially with the elderly woman's portrait looking on. But at this point, Ian would agree to make love anywhere, including the living room floor.

When they reached the double bed in the room that had become their love nest, Carly pulled down the spread. Then she turned to him and opened her arms, letting him know she was far from changing her mind.

This was the warm and willing woman he remembered, the one he'd nearly fallen heart over head for. He kissed her again, long and deep. As their tongues mated, a surge of desire shot through him, and he pulled her hips forward against his erection.

She moaned, then clutched at his shoulders, moving against him, making him wild with need. When he thought he might explode from the pent-up passion, he tore his mouth from hers. His breath came out in soft, ragged pants when he said, "You have no idea how badly I want you."

"Yes, I do. I want you, too. And even though—"

He placed his finger against her lips, stopping her from mentioning any second thoughts, any concerns. "Don't think about the past or worry about the future, honey. Just concentrate on the here and now. I want us to make love the way we used to."

Apparently, she did, too, because she began unbuttoning her blouse. Her breasts were much fuller than he remembered. Her pretty black lace bra could scarcely contain them.

He watched as she slid down the zipper of her jeans, and peeled the denim over her hips, revealing a pair of skimpy black lace panties. He'd never imagined that he could find a pregnant woman so damned sexy.

The swell of her baby bump was the sweetest and most amazing thing he'd ever seen. And when she stepped out of her black Wrangler jeans and kicked them aside, he placed his hand over the mound of her belly where their child grew. Then he looked into her eyes and smiled. "This is beautiful. *You're* beautiful. And it makes you more desirable than ever."

An "I love you" nearly rolled off his tongue, but he bit it back. The last thing he needed to do was to scare her away, even though he'd never actually realized the truth of those three little words until this very moment. He loved Carly. He wanted her. *Needed* her.

He removed his clothes, then slipped his arms around her waist. She skimmed her nails across his chest, sending a shiver through his veins and a rush of heat through his blood. Then she unsnapped her bra and freed her breasts, full and round, the dusky pink tips darker than he'd remembered, yet peaked and begging to be kissed.

He bent and took a nipple in his mouth, using his tongue and lips until she gasped in pleasure. Then he scooped her into his arms and placed her on top of the mattress. He wanted nothing more than to slip out of his boxers and feel her skin against his, but he paused for a beat and savored the angelic sight of the woman he was sorely tempted to offer marriage—if he thought she might agree.

He joined her on the bed, where they continued to kiss, to taste and to stroke each other until they were both wild and breathless and flinging their undergarments across the room.

When he rose up and over her naked body, she opened for him. He entered her slowly at first, this time without the need of a condom, relishing the feel of being inside her. But passion soon took over.

As her body responded to his, giving and taking, any reservations either of them ever had seemed to disappear. Nothing else mattered but this very moment and the pleasure they gave each other. When he felt her reach a peak and heard her cry out, he let himself go, releasing along with her in a sexual explosion.

As the last waves of their climax ebbed, Ian rolled to the side, taking Carly with him, holding her close. "It's like our bodies knew right where they'd left off."

"I know." She smiled and placed a hand on his chest. "We probably should talk about the future."

He wanted to object, to tell her to let it wait until morning—or next week. Or better yet, even after the baby came. But she was right. And he feared that making love had only complicated the issue.

As Carly lay in Ian's arms, fully sated, she realized how deeply she cared for him—and how hurt she'd be if he refused to give up his job at the Leaning R and support her quest to make a name for herself in the country music world.

She no longer expected him to sing with her, but if they were going to create a family together, they couldn't do it from the Leaning R, especially since the ranch might belong to someone else within a few months.

He drew her close and nuzzled her neck, a move that should have comforted her. Instead, it set off a sudden onslaught of bells and whistles.

This wasn't going to be easy. Where would they

live? How would they work things out so they could both fulfill their dreams?

Or would she be expected to give up hers?

She'd grown up as Charles Rayburn's daughter, a princess in many ways. But her life in the castle hadn't been very happy. Her father had rarely come to any school plays, award ceremonies or sporting events. He'd even missed her high school graduation. "I'm sorry, baby girl," he'd said over the telephone. "I have a critical business meeting I have to attend. But I'll add five thousand dollars to your trust account. Go shopping on me."

He hadn't always given her an excuse for his paternal absences, but when he did, they were always business related.

Then there'd been her mother—a country star who'd lit the stage with her dazzling smile and talent. But Carly had always remained in the shadows, watching her mother on TV or hearing her hits on the radio. She'd just nod when people said, "Aren't you a lucky girl." But she'd quit smiling by the time she was ten. It was hard enough to hold back the tears, let alone feign happiness.

Could Carly be content only to be known as Ian's wife or her child's mother?

She supposed she could if Ian didn't smother the dream of the little girl inside her.

Yet the longer she lay in bed with him, the harder it was to breathe. She couldn't foresee a future for them unless Ian was willing to compromise and give her the freedom she needed to be someone.

"Do you ever see yourself as a wife and mother?" he asked.

His words struck a chilling blow, and she realized she'd given him the wrong idea.

"Not the way you probably do."

Silence stretched across the mattress, creating a distance between them in spite of their embrace.

Making love, as good as it had been, as much as she'd needed to be in Ian's arms tonight, had been a mistake.

One she didn't dare make again.

Chapter Nine

Not wanting to lose the afterglow of their lovemaking, Ian suggested they discuss the future in the morning, and Carly agreed. They spent the night together, as had been their routine before, but sometime during the wee hours of the morning, she'd rolled to the far side of the bed, hugging her pillow instead of him.

He'd told himself not to give it much thought, but he'd slept like hell. Before dawn, he got up, dressed quietly and slipped out of the room, taking care not to wake her. But this time he wasn't heading out to do his morning chores, although he'd need to tend to those, too. He was going to check on Cheyenne.

The puppy had plenty of food and water, but she'd undoubtedly missed his company. So there was no telling what she'd chewed up or how many puddles or piles she'd left on the floor.

But as he tiptoed through the quiet ranch house, snuck out the back door in the darkness and headed for his cabin, he realized there was actually another reason for his stealthy departure. He wanted to avoid Carly.

Sure, they needed to talk. And maybe he should even level with her and tell her that he'd fallen in love with her. But he doubted she felt the same way about him. And he wasn't about to settle for a relationship in which one partner wasn't fully committed to the other. On his grandparents' ranch, he'd grown up in a loving household and seen firsthand how a good marriage worked. His grandparents had honored their wedding vows for nearly fifty years, and Ian didn't want anything less.

But Carly hadn't had the same loving example when she'd been a child, and he was afraid that when they finally broached the future, she'd decide to end their relationship again. He couldn't do anything about it if she chose to leave, but he wasn't going to let the baby go as easily.

When he opened the front door to the cabin that had been his home for the past three years, Cheyenne charged him, jumping up on her hind legs, whining and wagging her little stump of a tail in greeting.

What Ian wouldn't give to have Carly and their child greet his arrival like this, but that wasn't likely.

He loved Carly—and he would adore their son or daughter—but she didn't appear to want to create a family with him. At least, not the kind he'd always envisioned for himself. He tried to understand that it wasn't her so much as the childhood she'd had that influenced her thinking, but it was getting more and more difficult to make excuses for her.

Still, it was going to kill him to see her go on tour—which she seemed hell-bent on doing. But what other option did he have?

None that he could see, because he was every bit as determined to chart his own future as Carly was. And the paths they'd chosen weren't likely to cross.

A telephone rang, waking Carly from a sound sleep. The morning sun peeked through the slats in the blinds, but other than that, she had no idea what time it was. Or where she was.

She opened one eye and scanned the surroundings, suddenly recognizing the guest room and realizing that she was tangled up in the sheets alone. Apparently Ian had slipped out of bed earlier, which had usually been his habit. But this time… Well, things weren't the same anymore.

The phone rang again. Not her cell, but the old-style house telephone.

She rolled out of bed, still naked from the night of lovemaking, then hurried to the living room and snatched the receiver off the cradle. She managed to answer before the fourth ring.

It was Shannon Miller, Braden's mother.

"How's it going?" Carly asked, wondering why she'd called so early.

"My…uh…dad passed away a few hours ago."

Carly's heart dropped to her stomach. "Oh, no. I'm so sorry to hear that. Is there anything I can do?"

"Not that I can think of. Erik is here and has been handling everything."

Carly combed her fingers through her tousled hair. "All right, but please let me know if you need anything."

"Thanks, honey. I appreciate that. Could you please tell your brother?"

"Of course." At least, she'd try to get a hold of Jason. His cell reception in Mexico was sometimes sketchy.

After she said goodbye to Shannon, she dialed Jason's number. While it rang, she bit back a yawn and wondered what time it actually was.

She glanced at the fireplace mantel, looking for the antique clock, but it had already been packed away in one of the sealed boxes that lined the far wall. The house, she realized, had never looked so empty. As a rush of grief and loneliness swept through her, she wished she'd gotten dressed before placing the call.

"Hey, Carly," her older brother said. "What's up?"

Rather than blurt out her news, she decided to ease into it. "Are you and Juliana still in Mexico?"

"Yes, we're staying in a motel in a small town that's about a hundred miles south of Guadalajara. I'm glad you called. We found the twins."

"That's good news." Now maybe her brother and his new bride could come back to the States and start their lives together.

"Juliana and I were relieved to find them with the

nanny, but we'll have to brush up on our high school Spanish. They don't speak English."

Carly could see where communicating would be tricky and smiled. "Then they're lucky I wasn't the one to find them. I took French in school."

He laughed. "Yeah, we've come up with our own kind of sign language, so we're getting by."

"Then they weren't living in an orphanage?"

"No, they've been staying with the nanny, an older woman dad had hired. But she isn't happy with the setup. Her English isn't very good, either, but she made herself clear. She doesn't want to keep them any longer."

"Oh, no. Those poor kids."

"Apparently Dad's private investigator paid her for two months in advance and told her Dad would either send for her and the kids or pick them up as soon as he could. But he never called or showed up."

"Did she know that he was killed in a car accident, probably on his way to get them?"

"She does now. Apparently she's upset about not being paid for her services, so I gave her five hundred in cash. But I'll need to find a bank to get the rest of the money she says he owes her, although I suspect she's not being completely honest about the amount."

Carly ran a hand through her hair again, her finger catching on a tangle. "What are you going to do with the kids?"

"I'll bring them back with us. Fortunately, their paperwork seems to be in order. At least Dad managed to get that squared away."

"Does that mean you won't have any problem crossing the border with them?"

"We shouldn't. And apparently we found the nanny just in time. She'd already had the kids packed and ready to return to the orphanage."

"That's so sad. And pretty cold. What kind of woman is she?"

"A businesswoman, it seems."

Carly slowly shook her head. If the children didn't have anyone to love and care for them, no wonder her father had felt sorry for them and wanted to bring them to the States. "I hope the nanny didn't abuse or neglect them."

"They seem to be well fed and healthy. And we haven't seen any cuts or bruises. So my guess is that she did all right by them."

That was a relief. Her father wasn't the only one who'd had a soft spot for disadvantaged children. Of course, he'd always put his wallet where his heart was, making large donations to charities that funded various programs for kids.

He hadn't actually gotten personally involved, though. And that had been true with his own children. She wondered what made Camilla's twins different.

Had he known that Camilla was a single mother and that there wouldn't be anyone to look after her kids? That seemed likely.

"Will you tell Braden that I found them?" Jason asked.

"Yes, of course. But just so you know, his mother

called me a few minutes ago. His grandfather passed away during the night, so I told her I'd let you know."

"Oh, no. I'm sorry to hear that."

"It was expected."

"I know it was, but Mr. Miller was a good man—and more of a father to Braden than our dad ever was."

Jason had that right. And while she and her brothers had been as different from each other as the three mothers who'd borne them, they'd been raised by the same dad who'd provided for every financial need they'd ever wanted, often neglecting the emotional ones.

The line went silent for a moment. Then Carly asked, "When are you coming home?"

"In a day or two. But I have a couple of business issues to take care of in Houston, so I'll have to stop by the corporate office first."

"At Rayburn Enterprises?"

"No, at Rayburn Energy Transport. There's talk of a strike, and I'd like to settle things before they get out of hand. But I may have to be there for a while. I just hope Braden was able to find someone to adopt the twins. I can't keep them forever. Besides, I have plans to take Juliana on a real honeymoon."

Carly doubted that Braden had found anyone yet, and with his grandfather's passing, he probably wouldn't be searching for a while.

Gosh, she hoped Jason didn't ask her to take on the twins, especially when she had a baby of her own on the way.

For the briefest moment, she considered sharing her

baby news with her older brother, but she opted to hold off a little while longer. They hadn't been especially close in the past, although that seemed to be changing now that their dad was gone. But Jason might not like the idea that she and Ian weren't married, or that they hadn't decided where a baby would leave the two of them.

"I'll let you know when we get back to the States," Jason said.

"Okay. Take care."

When the call ended, Carly returned to the bedroom, her hand resting on her bare tummy. As long as she didn't announce she was expecting, she didn't have to think about the future and how the baby would fit into her plans.

And the longer she could put off discussing her future plans with Ian.

As the day wore on, Ian knew he couldn't avoid Carly indefinitely. He'd already checked all of the pastures as well as the pump he and the boys had fixed earlier, so there wasn't any other reason for him to stay away from the house.

When he finally rode into the yard, Carly stepped out onto the front porch as if she'd been waiting for him. She was dressed in a loose-fitting white sundress, the skirt billowing. Her pretty legs were bare—and so were her feet.

The breeze kicked up a strand of her hair, whisking it across her face, and she brushed it aside. She looked as pretty as a picture. Whether she knew it or not, she was a living, breathing part of the Leaning R. And he couldn't help thinking how nice it would be to return home to her each day.

As he dismounted, she approached him and his bay gelding, as though eager to talk. Had he misread her last night? Had she not been drawing away from him?

"Shannon called," she said. "Gerald Miller passed away last night."

"That's too bad." Ian swung down from his horse. "But he was pretty sick and in pain."

"They said he passed peacefully." The wind picked up another strand of her hair, and this time, when she swiped it aside, she tucked it behind her ear. "I just got back from the Miller ranch. I fixed Braden and his mom a casserole and baked a cake. I also offered to help in any way I can."

"That was nice. I'm sure they won't feel like cooking for a while."

"That's what I thought." She placed her hands on her hips and blew out a sigh. "While I was there, Braden told me that he's going to sign the listing agreement. So it looks like the Leaning R will go on the market within the next week."

"You're still going to sign, right?" Ian asked.

She nodded. "I can't run this place on my own. Besides, I'm not planning to stay in Brighton Valley forever." She studied him as though she was waiting for him to object or to bring up the baby, but he didn't do either.

"I'm sorry your family isn't going to keep the place," he said, lifting his hat and readjusting it over his mussed, sweat-dampened hair. "But I'm glad you all agreed to sell."

"Why? I'd think you'd be worried about losing your job or having to work for someone new."

Ian proceeded to remove the saddle from his bay gelding. "Did Jason tell you that Ralph Nettles had a buyer interested in purchasing the ranch?"

"Yes, he mentioned it. If that's true, then it should sell quickly, which I suppose is good."

Ian placed the saddle and blankets over the top rung of the corral. "Well, I'm the buyer Ralph Nettles was talking about."

Her brow furrowed, the news clearly taking her by surprise. "You?"

Apparently she still saw him as a simple cowboy, which ought to bother him, but how could it? He'd never revealed his life in Nashville. "Believe it or not, I've already got the offer ready to go."

Disbelief—or maybe distrust—twisted her expression. "Can you pull it off? I mean, my brothers are going to want top dollar, and I don't think they'll be willing to carry paper."

He didn't need them to extend him any kind of credit. He'd made some sound investments and still had plenty of royalties rolling in. "It just so happens that I have a little nest egg put aside."

Her brow furrowed deeper still, as she no doubt pondered what "little" meant to him.

What she didn't realize was that he could probably pay cash for the place—unless they were actually asking a lot more than it was worth. But he'd already gone over the figures with Mr. Nettles, and he figured it would work out okay.

"Well, then," she said, giving a little shrug, "I guess that's good news. I'd rather see the ranch go to you than to a stranger."

"You're still welcome to come home anytime you want. I'll keep the guest room ready for you." He offered her a smile, an olive branch of sorts.

"Thanks. I might take you up on that." Then she slowly turned and made her way back to the porch. As she placed her hand on the railing and her foot on the first step, she paused and turned around. "I forgot to mention that I talked to Jason and got an update from him."

That wasn't what he'd expected her to say, but apparently she had some news to share. "How's the search going?"

Carly told him about the twins, the money-minded nanny and the plan to return with the twins soon. After bringing him up to speed, she turned and continued into the house.

The fact that she hadn't mentioned eating dinner together didn't go unnoticed. But he wasn't going to make any speculations when it came to Carly. She had to do what she thought was right.

And so did he.

Carly felt a little dumbfounded as she returned to the house. Ian planned to buy the ranch?

The idea had blindsided her because she hadn't expected him to have saved up enough money for a sizable down payment. He seemed to think he had it all figured out, though.

She hoped he was right. Because even though his game plan seemed to come out of the blue, she actually preferred to have him take ownership rather than someone she didn't know.

But now he would be even more tied to Brighton Valley and the Leaning R than ever. So where did that leave her and the baby?

She'd hardly given her thoughts room to breathe when she heard her cell phone ring. The customized ringtone told her it was her mother.

After reaching her cell, which had been charging on the maple bureau in the bedroom, she answered the call. "Hi…" *Raelynn* nearly rolled off her mouth, but she opted for a belated "Mom."

Raelynn's voice came out in a rush. "Are you doing all right, honey? I had the weirdest dream last night. You know I never give that stuff much thought, but on the outside chance that something was wrong, I thought I'd better call."

"I'm fine. So whatever dream you had wasn't a premonition."

"That's good. I'd dreamt that you went for a ride on a pretty little pinto pony. But when it reared up, it turned out to be one of those rodeo horses your brother Braden raises on the Bar M. The crazy, snorting, red-eyed beast bucked you off, and you broke your neck. It was so real that I woke up in a cold sweat."

"Everything is okay here, but oddly enough, Braden's grandfather passed away last night."

Raelynn's breath caught. "Oh, that's too bad. What happened? Don't tell me he was thrown from a bronco and killed."

"No, he had cancer. He'd been fighting it for a while."

"What a shame. He seemed like such a nice man. I'd like to send flowers or something. When are the services?"

"On Wednesday. According to what Shannon said earlier today, it'll be a celebration of his life. They plan to hold it on the ranch."

"I'll make sure to order a nice spray of roses and have them delivered. I'm afraid David and I will be leaving for London the next day, and I'll be busy packing and having my hair and nails done."

"I'll tell Shannon you're sorry you had to miss it."

"Thank you, honey."

"I do have something to tell you, though." Carly bit down on her bottom lip, wondering how her mother would take the news, but she couldn't keep it a secret forever.

"What is it?"

"I'm pregnant." The line went still, and Carly sensed her mother's shock.

After several beats, she found her voice, "Oh, dear." Her tone indicated she'd just been given some disturbing news. Had she connected the dots to realize that meant she was going to be a grandmother? That ought to send her over the edge.

"I take it you didn't elope without telling me," Raelynn said. "Are you going to marry the baby's father?"

"I'm not sure. We haven't discussed it yet."

Raelynn blew out an exasperated sigh. "I suppose we can keep it quiet."

"We won't be able to keep it under wraps too long. I'm already nearly five months pregnant."

Raelynn clucked her tongue. "I can't believe you're just telling me now. David is up for reelection, and I'd hate to have it get out that my daughter is unwed and pregnant. It might put a real damper on his standing with conservative voters."

Great, Raelynn. Why don't we make this all about you? Carly didn't say what she was thinking, but then again, every hope, every dream she'd ever had, everything she'd ever done, had revolved around her mother's career and her convenience.

But Carly would be darned if she'd get married just to please Raelynn and the senator's potential voters. And she was rebellious enough these days to refuse to marry Ian, even if he asked her.

"I'm not sure what I plan to do about the baby's father," she said. "We can talk more about it when you get back from Europe."

"All right. But I hope you won't tell anyone in the meantime."

Like who? The paparazzi? The *Brighton Valley Gazette*? Or was she afraid Carly would announce it on Facebook, where the news networks might catch wind of it?

"For Pete's sake, Mom. Can't you be just a little supportive? My pregnancy might seem like a scandal to you, but I'm actually happy about having a baby."

As the words rolled off her lips, she realized they held some truth. "I just wish you'd be happy, too."

"I'm not unhappy," Raelynn said. "And I'm not a prude. Lord knows I've made mistakes, too."

Somehow, Carly didn't see her baby as a "mistake." And it grated upon her to think her mother did.

"It's just that the timing could be better," Raelynn added.

Granted, that was true. Carly would have preferred to have gotten married before she got pregnant. And it would be nice if she'd had a chance to establish her career before starting a family. That way, she would feel good about taking time off to be a real mother to her son or daughter.

"I'll tell you what," Carly said, "I'll do everything I can to save you and the senator from any undue embarrassment, even if that means staying out of your life until the baby reaches adulthood."

"Now, that's not what I meant, Carly. You don't have to be so testy."

Didn't she? This entire conversation only reminded her how lousy her childhood had been. And how little she'd actually mattered in her mother's world. Raelynn may have given up singing and performing, but she still lived on a stage of sorts.

But none of that mattered anymore. Carly was going to have a baby—one who was loved. And she'd be a much better mother than Raelynn had been.

"Let's talk more about this later, after we both have a chance to let the news set in. In the meantime, have a good trip. I'll talk to you when you get back." Then they said their goodbyes and disconnected the line.

Carly wasn't so sure that she actually would call her mother after the London trip. But she did need to talk to Ian. And there was no point in putting it off any longer. They had some planning and compromises to make. After all, the baby would be here in a little more than four months.

Carly went outside, determined to find Ian and have the discussion she'd meant to have this morning. It took nearly ten minutes, but she finally heard Cheyenne yipping at something or other. So she followed the sound to the back of the barn.

Ian was leaning against the corral, studying one of the mares, while the little cattle dog tried to herd a couple of butterflies that hovered near a patch of bluebonnets. He turned when he heard her approach.

"Got a minute?" she asked.

"Sure." He pushed away from the wooden rail and slid his hands into the front pockets of his jeans. He was a handsome yet formidable sight as he stood there, all muscle and sinew and...cowboy strong.

"I've been putting off talking about the baby," she said, "mostly because I've been trying to wrap my mind around the news. But don't get me wrong. I'm not unhappy about it."

"I'm glad to hear it. And for the record, I'm actually looking forward to being a father."

"That's good to know."

The gelding moved to the side, and Ian gave it a pat

on the rump. "I want you to know that you can live here while the baby is young."

She'd suspected he would offer that. But did he think she'd be content to be a rancher for the rest of her life?

"Are you suggesting I give up my dream?" she asked.

"No, I'm just throwing out the idea that you could postpone it a bit. At least, the big-time aspects. Keep in mind that Earl Tellis would let you perform anytime you want at the Stagecoach Inn. I know it's not your idea of stardom, but you'd be doing what you want to do until you moved on to something more glamorous."

Would performing in a local honky-tonk be enough for her?

"And Stu Jeffries loves your voice," Ian added. "He'd have you singing at all the community events."

He was probably right about that, but would she grow to resent the small-town life in time?

She feared that she might. But instead of speaking her fears, she lifted her foot and brushed her big toe against a clump of dandelions on the ground.

"I'd marry you in a heartbeat," Ian added. "Just so you know."

Her own heartbeat fluttered at the thought, even though it wasn't a real proposal. Still, a wedding would certainly please Raelynn, but Carly couldn't marry a man who'd only proposed to provide his child with a name and to make an honest woman out of her. She needed to know that she was loved unconditionally.

She struggled with the urge to admit that she loved him, that his offer, while sweet, hadn't been enough.

But she knew admitting those words would only lead to heartbreak, so she kept them to herself.

"The way I see it," Ian said, "we have a lot of options. I'd be happy to watch the baby while you go on the road."

She ought to be thankful to have his support, but she didn't like the idea of going anywhere and leaving the baby behind. Yet she also hated the thought of remaining on the ranch with him indefinitely. The dilemma was killing her.

"Why can't you just go on the road with me?" she asked. "You don't have to perform. You could watch the baby."

"I can't do that," he said. "You're asking me to be Mr. Carly Rayburn."

"No, I'm not."

"Either way, a baby doesn't belong on the road with a singing act. It isn't a good environment—the long hours, the touring, the various hotel rooms. And that's just the logistics. There are other factors, too."

"How do you know what it would be like on the road?"

Ian opened his mouth to speak, then shut it and slowly shook his head.

Maybe he realized any argument he came up with wouldn't hold water.

"I'll tell you what," Carly said. "Why don't we give ourselves time to think about the options?"

"All right. But don't toss out the marriage idea."

She'd remember his offer. But she couldn't marry a man who didn't love her to the moon and back.

Chapter Ten

Shannon and Braden planned a celebration of life for Gerald Miller at their ranch on Wednesday afternoon, where many of the longtime Brighton Valley residents could pay their respects to a man who'd been their friend and neighbor.

Carly had driven over to the Bar M earlier that morning so she could help them set up. She'd asked Ian if he wanted to go with her, but he said he'd meet her there later.

So far they hadn't talked any more about the baby or the future, but they would have to do so soon. Her blind determination to pursue her dream at all costs seemed to be weakening. In fact, she still held Molly Carmichael's card in her purse and had yet to call her about representing her. How could she, when she'd just learned she was pregnant? She had no idea what the future might bring and hadn't wanted to make any kind of commitment until she figured it out.

Surprisingly, she found herself actually wanting to stay on the Leaning R until the baby came. After that, she'd just have to take each day as it came.

The more Carly thought about that plan, the better she actually liked it. Last night while she'd watched TV, she'd seen a commercial about a new baby store that had opened in Wexler. It seemed only natural for her to think about cribs and rockers—and to wonder which bedroom she should fix up for the nursery.

And as she'd continued to nest in her mind, she hadn't thought once about singing on stage. Instead she'd found herself humming lullabies and wondering if Ian had been serious about writing one of his own. If he was, maybe he'd let her come up with the lyrics for whatever tune he created.

Now, however, she would have to focus on the work at hand—and on the tribute to Gerald Miller, the gruff but kindly man everyone had liked and respected.

Gerald Miller had been a champion bronc rider who'd competed in rodeos all over the country. After his retirement, he'd turned his sights on breeding and training cutting horses. He was a successful business-man in his own right, honest and fair.

Folks around these parts looked up to cowboys. They seemed to have a code of honor unique to them. And Gerald was no different. He had a strong work ethic and a love of family and community.

Ian, too, was the epitome of the honorable cowboy.

And she'd found herself considering more than once over the past few days that he'd make a good husband and father. But at this point, she wouldn't entertain any thoughts other than that.

When the doorbell rang, Carly left the caterers in the kitchen and volunteered to answer it. "I'll bet it's the florist with another delivery."

And she'd been right. The driver held a plant garden in one hand and a large bouquet in the other. "Where do you want these?"

Carly scanned the living room, which was already adorned with several arrangements. Then she reached for the potted plant. "I'll set this on the hearth. You can put the bouquet on the coffee table."

"You got it." The delivery boy did as she instructed, then added, "There's one more still in my van."

He went outside and returned carrying a large spray of roses that had been arranged in the shape of a cowboy boot.

Carly gazed at the flowers and the stand that came with it. Something like that must have cost a pretty penny, and she wondered who'd sent it.

She reached for the small card and read, "With deepest sympathy. Senator David Crowder and Raelynn Fallon."

"Where would you like this to go?" the young man asked.

The stand-up display was too large for the living room, especially with all the other arrangements set out. "It should go in the backyard, near the horse arena, where the celebration will take place. But I'll take it."

"Thanks." He set the stand on the floor, then reached for the clipboard he'd tucked under his arm. "Can I get you to sign for this?"

After scratching out her name, Carly carried the spray outside, where several other large arrangements had been placed already. She found a spot for her mother's flowers, but before placing them, she took one last look at the large, colorful floral boot. It was a fitting arrangement for a man who'd been a true cowboy in every sense of the word.

As Carly started back to the house, Braden came out of the barn. He was dressed in black jeans, a white cotton shirt and a bolo tie. Talk about real cowboys—her brother also fit the image to a tee.

She hadn't had a chance to speak to him yet, so she crossed the yard and met him near the vegetable garden his grandpa had planted each spring.

"How are you holding up?" she asked.

"I'm doing okay. We were expecting it—and Grandpa had taken care of all the financial issues. Having his affairs in order has made everything easier."

"He was a good man," Carly said. "I'm sorry you lost him so soon."

"I guess we're never ready for a loved one to pass on." Braden blew out a sigh. "Thanks for coming early to help out today. My mom and I really appreciate it."

She offered him a smile. "That's what sisters are for."

A crooked grin tugged at his lips. "Yeah, maybe so."

"That reminds me," Carly said, "Jason and Juliana

will be coming back with the twins soon. Have you had any luck finding them a home?"

"No, not yet. I talked to Pastor Steuben at the Brighton Valley Community Church last week. He was going to look into it for us, but as far as I know, he hasn't found anyone yet."

"I guess it won't be easy to find someone willing to take on two kids, especially when they don't speak English."

"You're probably right. But I've got my fingers crossed."

Carly did, too. The poor kids had been through a lot already—losing their mother and their grandfather, spending time in an orphanage and then with a nanny who seemed to care more about finances than children. Now they were being uprooted again and moved to a different country where they would have to learn a new language. They'd also have to adjust to family life with strangers.

"On the upside," Braden said, "I stopped by Nettles Realty and signed the paperwork to list the Leaning R yesterday. From what I understand, Ralph still needs your and Jason's signatures, but he seems to think it's already as good as sold."

"I'll see Ralph and sign on Monday. I have a doctor's appointment that afternoon, so I'll be in town."

Braden furrowed his brow. "Is something wrong? I know you were sick while you were in San Antonio. You're not still dealing with that, are you?"

She was tempted to skate around the issue by telling him it was just a checkup, which it was. But there really was no use in keeping the news from him. "Actually, it's nothing to worry about. I'm just pregnant."

Braden flinched. "Boy, I didn't see that coming."

"Neither did I."

He glanced at her waistline, which was hidden behind the loose beige top she wore over a pair of black stretch pants. Then he asked, "Who's the father?"

She couldn't very well hold back that information, either. "Granny's foreman—Ian McAllister."

Braden seemed to give that some thought, then asked, "Does he know?"

She nodded. "He seems to be happy about it, but we're still trying to figure out how we're going to coparent. He offered to marry me, but I'm not so sure that's a good idea. I think he just made the offer because he's an honorable guy."

"Don't you want to get married?" Braden asked.

Not if they weren't crazy in love with each other. And although she had come to the conclusion that she might feel that way, it had to be a two-way street, and she wouldn't settle for less.

"Like I said, the future is still up in the air." She tucked a strand of hair behind her ear. "And you may as well know, Ian is the one who's interested in purchasing the Leaning R."

"That's what Ralph told me. And to be honest, I like the guy and have no problem with him buying the ranch. But where would a cowboy get that kind of money?"

"Ian said he's got it. Heck, maybe he has a trust fund like us." Even as she said it, she doubted that was the case—it didn't fit with what he'd told her about his family.

"The down payment alone is pretty hefty," Braden said. "And then he'll need the money to buy more cattle as well as to hire extra hands."

Carly hadn't thought about the startup funds Ian would need. "He mentioned having a small nest egg, but maybe he does have an inheritance of some kind."

"He seems pretty levelheaded," Braden said. "But I hope he isn't just dreaming about being able to make a purchase like this."

"No, I think he's serious."

Yet she couldn't help wondering the same thing. Could Ian actually come up with enough money to buy the ranch? Or was he chumming her?

He knew how she felt about selling the place. Was he trying to tempt her to stay with him?

"With the baby coming," Braden said, "maybe he's hoping you'll throw in your third from the proceeds, which would allow him the start-up funds he'll need."

Braden had a point. If Carly threw in her third, he'd only need to purchase the other 66 percent.

But Ian had never given her reason to believe he was using her for any reason. So she slowly shook her head. "No, he wouldn't expect me to do that."

Still, as the seeds of suspicion had sprouted, she cut them off at the root. There was no reason to believe Ian was pulling a fast one and trying to rope her into a situation she didn't want to be in. Her father might have pulled a stunt like that, but Ian wouldn't.

"I guess we'll find out soon enough," Braden said. "Once you and Jason sign the listing agreement, the ranch will be on the market. And then we can see what kind of an offer Ian makes."

And what kind of man he really was, she supposed.

"How soon do you think Jason will be able to sign the paperwork?" Braden asked.

"Within the next couple of days, I would guess."

Braden stroked his chin. "Do you think he and Juliana would consider keeping the twins—at least for a while?"

"That's a lot of responsibility for newlyweds to take on," Carly said.

"Maybe you can take them until we find a permanent home."

"Me?" Carly raised her hand, palm out. "Oh, no. Don't even go there. I wouldn't be any good with kids."

"Who says?" Braden smiled, then added, "Besides, you'd better get some practice if you'll be having one of your own."

That was true. She placed her hand on her tummy, which seemed to be growing bigger each day. She was just beginning to wrap her heart and mind around the changes taking place in her life. But she wasn't ready to add non-English-speaking twins to the list.

At the sound of an approaching vehicle, Braden said, "Speak of the devil. Here comes your baby daddy now."

Devil?

Again, Carly shook off her suspicion. Ian had been nothing but sweet and supportive. How could she possibly think he had any ulterior motives?

* * *

Ian arrived at the Bar M early. As he pulled into the drive, he spotted Carly and Braden talking in the yard.

He'd barely climbed from his truck when Braden's mother walked outside with a well-dressed man in his mid to late forties and joined them.

Ian was struck by how pretty Shannon Miller was. He'd never seen her fixed up before, with makeup on and with her brown hair soft and loose around her shoulders. If he didn't know better, he'd think she was Braden's older sister.

When Ian approached and offered his condolences, Shannon introduced her friend Dr. Erik Chandler. "He's been incredibly supportive these past few weeks. I don't know what I'd do without him."

The doctor slipped his arm around her waist, making a show of solidarity.

Ian liked seeing that. His grandparents leaned on each other through the good times and the bad. He'd noticed them talking in soft whispers, eyes glimmering and lips quirked in a smile. And he'd seen them cry together when their dog Buddy had died. To this day, they held hands when they took their afternoon walk.

He hoped Carly would learn that she could lean on him as the months wore on—or even the years. With a baby on the way, their lives would be entwined forever.

"Erik hired a caterer to fix the food, to set it out and to clean up afterward," Shannon said. "So there isn't much for us to do now except wait for people to arrive."

Dr. Chandler gave her a gentle squeeze. "You've been through enough already. And you've carried a heavy load for a long time. You don't need to worry about making sure everyone else is taken care of on a day like this."

Their smiles and his gentle touch implied they were more than just friends. If so, Ian was happy for her. From what Granny had told him, she really hadn't dated after Braden was born. And he'd found that to be sad.

"When things settle down," Shannon said, "Erik is going to take me to Hawaii for a vacation."

At that, Braden brightened. "I'm glad, Mom. You've spent your entire life looking out for me, Grandpa and the ranch. And that's not to mention all the time you poured into the church. You've always focused on others, so it's time you took a vacation and enjoyed yourself."

"Thanks for understanding, honey." Shannon placed a loving hand on Braden's sleeve. "For the time being, we'd better focus on getting through today."

A car sounded in the distance, and they turned to see who would be the first to arrive.

Ian took the opportunity to steal a glance at Carly, but instead of looking at the approaching vehicle, she was studying the older couple as intently as he'd been. Their friendship—or whatever they might call their particular relationship—was warm and loving as well as enviable.

In fact, their bond appeared to be the kind a couple made after supporting each other through life's ups and downs. Could she see that some relationships could be loving and strong?

As Carly continued to watch Shannon and Erik, Ian could have sworn he spotted a longing in her eyes. He wanted to assure her, to tell her to give him and her time and a chance to become a couple and a family.

But now wasn't the time, and this wasn't the place.

On Monday morning, Carly told Ian she was going to shop for baby furniture so she could fix up a nursery in what had once been Granny's sewing room.

He was relieved to hear of her decision and as much as he wanted to go with her, he didn't want to crowd her, especially since she planned to stick around for a while. So he was content to let her go alone.

Besides, he had plenty lined up to do today. Todd and the boys were going to start on the new fence he wanted to build in the south forty, and he figured it was best if he rode out with them.

By noon, they'd measured the field he planned to enclose, and he'd lined the teens up to start digging post holes. He probably should have waited until the property was officially his, but he wanted a place to keep the new calves he planned to buy.

While the hands took a lunch break, he rode back to the house to order the lumber and material they would need. He'd no more than entered the yard when he spotted a sleek, black limousine parked near the house.

He swore under his breath. There was only one person who could have arrived in a luxury car like that, and he braced himself for a strained reception as the chauffeur opened the door for Felicia Jamison.

"Just look at you," the red-haired country music star

said as she exited the limo. "I never would have believed it if I hadn't seen it for myself. Mac McAllister—in all his dusty, cowboy glory."

Ian rested a hand on the pommel, but he remained in the saddle. "I might have shaken off the dirt from my boots and cleaned up if I'd known you were stopping by."

"I certainly would have given you fair warning—if you would have left me a phone number or a forwarding address." She splayed her manicured hands on her hips. "If I didn't know better, I'd think you had been trying to avoid me for the past three years."

Damn. Why couldn't she have just let him be?

He bit back his frustration as well as his disappointment at seeing her. "Why would I do that? You're the prettiest stalker I've ever met. And the most famous."

"Actually," Felicia said as she approached him and the bay gelding he rode, "I let you slip off my radar for a while. But I need another big hit, and you're the only one who's ever been able to write with my voice and style in mind."

That was a fact. It had been his music and lyrics that had sent her to the top of the charts time and again. And she hadn't had an album go platinum since he ended their relationships—both personal and professional.

"I didn't think you were serious when you said you didn't want to perform anymore. But I realize now that you meant it back then."

He still meant it.

"But, Mac," she implored, "you don't have to go on

tour with me anymore. You can write songs here. And just to make the offer more tempting, I'll pay you twice the going rate if you'll come up with something special for me to sing in Los Angeles next month."

"I'm sorry, Felicia, but I'm not interested in furthering your career."

She stiffened. "You certainly hold a grudge."

"You're wrong. I let the past go years ago, but that doesn't mean I didn't learn a lesson along the way."

She offered him that little pout that used to work its charm on him. "Performing with me wasn't that bad, and you know it."

The hell it wasn't. He'd had to down several shots of tequila just to get through each day—a bad habit that might have become much worse, if he'd let it. But he bit back his objection.

"You can play rancher all you want," she added. "All you need to do is write one or two songs a year for me. With your talent and my voice, we'll go platinum again. I know it as sure as I'm standing here looking at you."

The anger and resentment he'd held toward her had disappeared a long time ago, but not his mistrust. And that alone had been enough for him to bow out of the public eye forever.

Felicia eased closer and placed her hand on the gelding's neck. "Come on, Mac. Climb down from there and let's talk about this on even ground."

There'd never been a level playing field between them, and it had taken Ian a while to learn that the fun-loving country girl on stage wasn't the real Felicia.

He didn't like being pressured, as had become Felicia's habit. It had only worked on him at first—until he knew the real woman behind the glossy red hair and big blue eyes. He soon got sick and tired of the energy it took to deal with all her demands, so he'd dug in his boots, which had frustrated her to distraction.

About the time he decided to cut bait and find a new band, she'd gotten pregnant. He hadn't been able to leave then. And for a couple of weeks, he'd thought they'd have to see a counselor so they could work things out. At least, that had been the idea until she'd chosen to abort the baby.

"Mac, honey." Her Southern twang deepened. "I know you haven't quit singing or playing. Or writing music, for that matter. It's in your blood. And strumming your guitar is how you wind down at night. You probably have a slew of new songs all ready to go."

He merely stared at her, yet he didn't swing down from his horse. He knew where this was going. She'd cozy up to him and make it sound as if they were long lost lovers who'd just stumbled upon each other. But this wasn't a chance meeting. She'd sought him out—probably thanks to the performances Carly had insisted they take part in recently. But he wouldn't give her the satisfaction of dismounting and meeting her at her level.

"You plannin' to make that little blonde a star?" she asked.

So he was right. She'd seen photos of him and Carly, probably on those damned posters the mayor had printed and stuck up all over the county.

"Nope. I'm not making anyone a star—nor am I helping anyone remain on top of the charts."

"I see." Felicia took a couple steps back. "You must be sleeping with her."

The assumption, which came out as an accusation, raked over him, but he wouldn't give her the pleasure of a reaction. "That's none of your business, Felicia. You moved on a long time ago."

"A girl can make a mistake, can't she?"

"Didn't you hear me? I'm *not* interested. I'm not about to repeat the past or work you into my future."

She crossed her arms again and shifted her weight to one hip. "That's a shame. You're wasting your talent."

Ian remained in his saddle, looking down at her. He'd seen her snub other musicians and singers on occasion, and it served her right to be on the other side of a brush-off.

"Don't you miss it?" she asked, her twang nearly nonexistent now. "The excitement, the glamour, the bright lights, the roar of the fans?"

"Nope. I don't miss it a bit." That wasn't exactly true. He still felt the magic of creating a brand-new tune and finding just the right words to go with it. But it had been nice to watch a crowd's reaction when his words and music struck something deep in their hearts.

"That blonde girl," Felicia almost spit out. "What's her name? Carly something? She probably thinks she's hit the big time now that she's met you."

"She knows better."

But Carly didn't really know who Ian was. The other day she'd asked him how he knew what it was like on the road. He could have revealed himself then, but he'd decided to wait until they came up with a satisfactory game plan for raising a child together.

At the time, he'd been afraid that, if Carly knew his true identity, she'd really pressure him. And he hadn't been about to let her force his hand. But it was time to tell her now.

In the meantime, he had to get rid of Felicia.

"I'm sorry, but I've gotta go. I'm meeting some hands out in the south forty. So you'll have to forgive me for leaving. I'm sure your driver can get this vehicle turned around on his own."

Then he jabbed his heels into the gelding's flanks and rode off, hoping Felicia would leave just as quickly.

Chapter Eleven

On her drive back to the ranch, Carly turned the radio up and sang a duet with Martina McBride. She hadn't been in this good of a mood for a long time.

She was pleased with her baby furniture purchase, which would be delivered to the ranch next week. Yet a single shopping spree hadn't appeased her desire to nest. If anything, it only made her want to start turning the old sewing room into a nursery as soon as possible.

If she'd had more time before her doctor's appointment this afternoon, she would've swung by the hardware store to look at paint samples as well as the fabric shop so she could choose the perfect print for the new curtains she planned to sew herself.

Imagine that. She was actually getting excited about having a baby. And in just an hour or so, she hoped to learn whether she would have a boy or a girl. The doctor hadn't had time for the ultrasound at her last visit, but it was scheduled for today.

She probably should have driven straight to the clinic, but she decided to stop by the ranch first so she could tell Ian what she'd done. She knew he'd be glad to hear that she was looking forward to getting a nursery ready for their child. And that she was even considering the possibility of making a home together.

Of course, she wouldn't agree to marriage unless he could convince her that he truly loved her. But who knew what time would bring?

While at the house, she planned to freshen up and maybe change into one of her new tops and a pair of comfy, loose-fitting jeans before heading to her appointment. The slacks she had on today were too snug and so was the blouse, even though she'd left the last button undone.

If Ian was around, she would invite him to go with her to the doctor's office. He'd probably like to see the ultrasound of their baby.

Since things had been up in the air before, she hadn't mentioned the test or the appointment to him. But now that they were… Well, not that they'd made any major decisions about their future, but they seemed to be falling into their Mommy and Daddy roles. And learning the sex of their baby together seemed like the right thing to do.

As she drove down the long, graveled drive to the Leaning R, she spotted a black limousine parked near the front porch, and her grip on the steering wheel tightened.

Had her mother come to visit? Raelynn would be the type to drive up in a limo. But she was supposed to be in London, so it couldn't be her.

The limo was turning around, as if leaving the house, but as Carly arrived, the driver pulled over. So she parked her pickup next to it.

Her dad used to own a limousine, which was a corporate vehicle now. Maybe Jason and Juliana had arrived in it. However, the Rayburn car had personalized license plates, so it couldn't be them. Well, not unless Jason had rented a limo after he arrived at the airport.

There was only one way to find out who it was. So she climbed from the pickup, leaving her shopping bag in the cab. She grabbed her purse and shut the door, just as the chauffeur exited the limo and proceeded to let his passenger out.

Carly watched an attractive redhead step out wearing snazzy cowboy boots, designer jeans and a denim jacket with a load of fancy sparkles. Dressed like that and riding in style meant she had big bucks.

As the redhead turned and faced the pickup, recognition dawned, and Carly's breath caught. What in the world was Felicia Jamison doing here?

Had Raelynn set up some kind of surprise for Carly? Had her mother actually used her connections to give her daughter's career a boost?

Carly had told Raelynn that she didn't need her help, but she wouldn't have objected if her mother had been insistent.

"Hi there," Carly said as she closed the pickup door and smiled. "What can I do for you?"

Felicia crossed her arms and, wearing a slight grin, gave Carly a once-over. "So you're the singer Mac hooked up with."

"Mac? I'm afraid I don't know who you're talking about."

"Mac McAllister, my old guitarist and song writer."

Carly blinked, hoping to catch up quickly and to connect the dots. "Do you mean *Ian* McAllister?"

"That's his given name, but he goes by Mac in music circles."

Music circles? Carly's head began to spin as if she were going to have another fainting spell, but it was just her thoughts swirling in her head.

"I…uh…" Carly nodded toward the barn. "His truck is here, so I suspect he's out in the south pasture. He said something about digging post holes and building a fence."

Felicia unfolded her arms and placed her hands on her denim-clad hips—her tight jeans a size two, no doubt. She wore gold bangles and a diamond bracelet on her wrist, and her fingernails sported a French manicure with square tips.

"I haven't heard you sing," Felicia said, "but rumor has it you're good. And that you might be trying to keep it a secret that you're Raelynn Fallon's daughter."

Rumor had it? And how had this woman known about Carly's connection to Raelynn? It's not like Carly threw her mother's name around.

But Ian knew. And right now, Carly would like to

throttle the quiet cowboy who'd failed to tell her he had music industry contacts of his own.

"I can see by the look in your eye that it's true," Felicia said. "How is your mama, now that she's retired and jet-setting with the senator?"

Carly knew she'd have to wipe the dumbfounded look off her face or she'd feel even more foolish than she did already. "What do you want with… Ian?"

"Well, apparently, he's already involved with… someone else, so I'll settle for just a musical reunion."

The story kept getting worse. Ian not only used to sing with Felicia, but he'd slept with her, too?

A flood of betrayal threatened to knock Carly off her feet, but she stood as tall as her five-foot-two frame would allow. "I guess you'll just have to talk to Ian— or rather, Mac—about that."

He'd had a hundred chances to level with her, but he'd never said a word. Wasn't that the same as lying?

"Actually," Felicia said, "I've already talked to him. He rode off a few minutes ago."

Apparently Felicia hadn't just arrived. She'd been about to leave. Carly wanted to tell her to climb back in that limo and hit the road because right now she wanted to be alone so she could have a good cry. Or maybe so she could kick something—or some*one*.

"Well, I'd better go," Felicia said. "It was nice meeting you."

Was it? Carly wasn't so sure, but she feigned a smile. "Same here."

"I'll leave you with one bit of advice, though," Felicia said.

Carly stiffened, and her stomach knotted. "What's that?"

"Be careful, hon. It's all fun and games with Mac until he gets you pregnant. Then he'll expect you to give it all up and settle down."

Felicia's parting shot struck Carly like a wallop to the chest. Sure, she'd started nesting and had considered settling down, at least a bit. But she'd thought that had been her idea.

Had Ian gotten her pregnant on purpose? They'd used protection, but had he known those condoms might fail? Had he planned to have her move in with him on the Leaning R all along?

Worse yet, maybe he expected her to use her share from the ranch proceeds to help him buy cattle and hire more hands.

Ian had often accused Carly of "working" him, but had it been the other way around all along?

As Felicia turned and headed back to the limousine, emotion clogged Carly's throat. She couldn't utter a goodbye or—what seemed even more fitting—a good riddance.

Ian had no more than reached the section of land that bordered the county road when he spotted Carly driving back to the ranch. If Felicia hadn't left yet, she'd probably stick around a bit longer now.

Damn. He didn't want those two talking without him present. Who knew what tale Felicia might concoct in an effort to get back at him? He'd seen her in action before and knew how she could morph from country sweetheart to jealous vamp in no time at all. He had to get back to the ranch. And fast.

He rode into the yard, just as the limo driver was opening the passenger door for Felicia to get back inside. But Carly was parked and standing outside her truck. Obviously the two had already had words.

When Felicia noticed that Ian had returned, she paused in midstep, then turned to face him, grinning as smugly as a fat-cheeked cat with yellow tail feathers poking out from its clenched lips.

Carly, on the other hand, appeared ready to bolt.

"I see you two have already met," he said as he dismounted.

Carly didn't utter a response, but she didn't have to. Her wounded gaze gave her emotions away. And why wouldn't she be hurt? He should have told her about his past earlier. There was no telling what kind of a spin Felicia had put on things.

"You're back," Felicia said. "That's nice. I'd love to stay and chat, but I have a business meeting in Houston, then I'm flying back to Nashville."

That was good news, assuming she was being honest. But the damage had already been done, and the smirk on her face told him she knew it. Now he'd have to do his best to rectify whatever havoc she'd created. But first he needed to make a point, especially with Carly looking on. "Just for the record, Felicia, you and I were done years ago. And I'm not up for a reunion of any kind."

"It's a shame you feel that way, Mac. But you know me. I've never been one to take no for an answer. Who knows what the future might bring." Felicia motioned to her driver. "Let's go." Then she climbed into the back of the limousine.

Mac led the horse to the corral, opened the gate and let him in. By the time he'd secured the latch, Felicia was well on her way down the drive.

On the other hand, Carly was still standing in the yard, her arms crossed, waiting for an explanation.

"I'm sorry," he said. "I should have been more up-front with you."

"You *think*?" Her sarcasm rang in the air. "Holding back information like having a music career and working with Felicia Jamison was just as dishonest as a flat-out lie."

He had that coming. And the fact that he valued honesty above all else sent his regret and guilt reeling.

"I'm not sure what Felicia told you," he said, "but just so you know, she's not the sweet little Southern gal she projects on the stage and in the media. She has a mean and vindictive streak she's good at hiding."

Carly placed her hands on her hips. "And just what kind of persona did *you* project on stage, *Mac*?"

He gave a half shrug. "I only wanted to play the guitar."

She swept her hand across the yard. "And now you do, except you're entertaining a puppy and a bunch of cows."

"I entertained you a time or two."

"Ain't that the truth." She clucked her tongue and slowly shook her head. "Do you have any idea how badly it hurts to know that you couldn't trust me enough to level with me?"

"I can only imagine—and I apologize yet again. But just so you know where I'm coming from, Felicia wasn't content to let me be myself. She tried to manage every minute of my life, and I got tired of it. I needed a complete break."

"You were so tired of it that you couldn't share the truth with me? We were lovers, Ian. And you're the father of my baby. Didn't I deserve to know?"

"Yes, you did. But the more you pushed me to perform with you, the more I held back. I figured you'd only press me harder."

He waited for her to soften, for her to give him some kind of clue that she might forgive him. But she glanced at her bangle wristwatch, then shook her head. "I can't do this." She walked to her pickup and opened the door. "I *won't* do it."

"What do you mean?" he asked. "Where are you going?"

"To see Dr. Connor." Then she slid behind the wheel, started the ignition and sped off, blowing gravel and dust behind her.

Why was she going to the doctor again? Was she sick? Or was she having a pregnancy complication?

A shudder of apprehension shook him to the bone. All he could think about was the day Felicia had gone to the clinic to end her pregnancy.

Surely that's not what Carly had in mind. She wasn't anything like Felicia. But she was hurt and angry. And he felt compelled to chase after her and make sure she didn't do something they'd both regret.

Carly was in tears before she pulled onto the county road and headed for the clinic. What in the world was she going to do now?

Ian wasn't the man he'd led her to believe he was. Besides that, all along he'd had the connections to open doors for her. Not that she would have wanted him to, but why hadn't he trusted her with the truth about his past?

Her cell phone rang, and she glanced at the number display on her dashboard. It was Ian, but she wasn't up to talking to him now. She let his call go to voice mail.

Moments later, another call came in. Assuming it was Ian again, she was about to shut off the phone completely when she spotted the incoming number and realized it was her brother.

She sniffled, then answered. "Hi, Jason. How's it going?"

"Just fine. But I have some news for you. *Big* news."

Not as big—or as messy—as hers was going to be. "What's up?"

"You know Camilla's twins?"

"What about them?"

"Are you sitting down?"

She rolled her eyes. "Come on. Don't keep me hanging."

"I told you that their paperwork was in order," he began. "But I hadn't looked it over until Juliana and I were getting ready to head to the airport with them."

"Was something wrong with their passports?"

"That depends on how you look at it."

"Okay, cut to the chase, Jason. I have an appointment in about ten minutes, and I don't have time for guessing games."

"Do you remember telling me that you always wished you'd had a sister?" He chuckled softly. "Well, you have one. And she's seven years old. You have a little brother, too."

Carly was so stunned she could barely find her voice. He had to be pulling her leg. Or else there was some mistake. "Are you kidding me?"

"Nope. It's true."

Jason had never lied to her before, but she still had trouble believing this. "Did Dad adopt them?"

"I don't think so. He's listed as their father on the birth certificates."

"Maybe they were forged or something. Dad could have paid to have someone create phony paperwork so he could bring them across the border more easily."

"That's not likely. The kids were born in San Diego, and those certificates aren't copies. They're legit. It's all there in black and white. Their parents are Camilla Cruz de Montoya and Charles Rayburn."

A horn tooted behind Carly, and when she glanced in the rearview mirror, she spotted a Ford sedan on her tail. The driver honked again, then sped up and passed her. When she looked at her speedometer, she realized she'd slowed almost to a stop.

She accelerated, then said, "So you're saying that Dad had another family in Mexico."

"Apparently so. That has to be why he was so determined to get those kids back to the States."

"Wow. I don't know what to say. I'm speechless."

"So are we. But we'll be heading back to Houston with them later today. I'll have some work to take care of at the office, but we need to schedule another family meeting. In the meantime, Juliana and I will keep them with us in my condo in Houston."

"Have you told Braden yet?" she asked.

"No, I called you first, but he's next on the list."

Carly glanced in the rearview mirror and noted that there weren't any more impatient drivers behind her. Then she blew out a sigh. "I'm still having a hard time believing this."

"While you try to figure it out, you might want to take a speed course in conversational Spanish."

Great. She'd finally gotten the little sister she'd always wanted, only nearly twenty years too late. And to make matters worse, they wouldn't be able to communicate.

"But now we have another problem," Jason said. "Since we know who the kids are, finding someone to adopt them isn't going to be the answer. Not when they're our blood kin."

He meant they'd have to figure out which sibling was going to step up and raise them. But that wasn't going to be easy. It had taken them months to agree to sell the Leaning R, mostly because they'd never been close—thanks to their father's two marriages and various affairs that left the half siblings feeling more like strangers than kin.

And while she had to admit that things had gotten better between her, Braden and Jason after their father died, and that the family dynamics had suddenly changed—big-time—they were still getting to know and respect each other.

And speaking of the Rayburns multiplying like bunnies… "Hey, listen. I have a doctor's appointment. I have to hang up or I'll be late. Call me when you get to Houston. I have some news for you, too."

"You can't tell me now?"

She'd rather have some time to let her thoughts settle after that blowup with Ian. "No. I'll talk to you later this evening or tomorrow morning."

Then she ended the call, just as she pulled into the clinic's parking lot. Maybe she'd better sit in the car and listen to some calming music. If the nurse took her blood pressure right now, it would probably be sky-high.

Chapter Twelve

Ian had just brushed down the gelding—the fastest cool down he could allow the horse. Then he went to the cabin and grabbed the keys to his truck, hoping he wouldn't be too late to catch up with Carly.

He'd no more than opened the door of his vehicle when Todd rode in with the boys. He was leading Jesse Ramirez's mare, while the seventeen-year-old sat in the saddle and held on to his left hand.

"What happened?" Ian asked.

"Jess had a run-in with a hammer and a stubborn nail," Todd said. "I think he might have busted his hand."

Jesse appeared more disappointed and angry at himself than hurt. "It was my fault. I can't believe I was so stupid. I sure hope it isn't broken."

"These things happen," Ian said.

"I know," Jesse said. "I just wish it hadn't happened to me. Maybe, if I put some ice on it, the swelling will go down and I'll be good as new tomorrow."

Jason Rayburn had hired the kids, all football players for Brighton Valley High School, and Ian hadn't liked the idea. But they all had busted their butts to do a good job, saying that ranching during the summer gave them a harder workout than the gym.

They'd all bulked up in the past month or so, which had been their plan, along with earning some spending money.

"I didn't mean to let you down," Jesse said. "I know how much work you have to do around here."

"Don't worry about me. I have to cut out now anyway." In truth, Ian was more concerned about the kid than a day's work. He didn't want to see Jesse miss the opening football game. This was his senior year, and he was hoping to earn a college scholarship.

"Let's call it a day," Ian told Todd. "Can you take Jesse to the ER to have an X-ray?"

Todd lifted his hat, then readjusted it on his head. "Sure thing, boss."

Ian was grateful for that. Normally, he'd be the one taking an injured employee for medical treatment. But having Todd do it would allow him to follow Carly to the clinic and make peace with her. "I've got to run into town," he told Todd. "Call me and let me know what the doctor has to say about Jesse's hand. I'll see you tomorrow."

Then he climbed into his truck and took off. All the while, he planned what he'd say to Carly.

He'd swear that he would never lie to her again—or withhold information. But there was one thing he'd neglected to confess.

He loved her with all his heart. And he was willing to lay his dreams on the line if that's what it took to create the family he'd always wanted.

He just hoped he wasn't too late—in more ways than one. God willing, he'd catch up with her before she made any foolish decisions.

And before she decided he wasn't the kind of man she could trust.

As he drove, he whipped out his cell phone. He dialed 411 and requested the number to Dr. Connor's office. When the receptionist answered, he asked for the address and directions. Apparently, the doctor's practice was located near the Brighton Valley Medical Center.

Twenty minutes later, he pulled into the parking lot and spotted Carly's pickup.

He entered the redbrick building that housed various medical offices and made his way to Dr. Connor's waiting room, which was nearly full. He noticed several mothers with children as well as a middle-aged man reading *Sports Illustrated*. But Carly was nowhere in sight.

"Excuse me," he said to the receptionist, prepared to stretch the truth. "I'm late. I'm supposed to meet Carly Rayburn here. I'm the father of her baby."

The matronly blonde smiled. "She was just called back to see the doctor. But I can take you to her."

"That would be great. Thanks." Ian had no idea how Carly would react when he crashed her visit with the doctor, but he wouldn't think about that now. He had to see her, to convince her to talk to him, and it couldn't wait a minute longer.

"She's right back here," the receptionist said as she led Ian to exam room three. She knocked lightly on the door. "Dr. Connor?"

"Yes?" another female voice said.

"The baby's father is here."

"Send him in. He's just in time."

Just in time for what? Ian was hesitant to enter the room, but Carly hadn't uttered an objection.

As he stepped inside, he spotted Carly stretched out on the exam table, her belly exposed. Something slick and wet was smeared on her skin, and the doctor was running some thingamajig over the swell of her belly. Apparently she was so transfixed by the image on a small screen that he practically slipped into the room unnoticed.

"That's the heartbeat," the doctor said. "It's strong and steady. Can you hear it?"

All Ian could hear was a *whoosh-whoosh-whoosh* sound, but he zeroed in on the black-and-white screen Carly was studying intently.

And then he saw it. Arms and legs. It was their baby. His heart lurched.

"Everything looks great," the doctor said.

As Ian watched the screen, the little feet kicked.

And one hand moved toward its mouth, providing a thumb to suck on.

Ian was awestruck and eased closer to watch his and Carly's baby. The image was grainy, but it was still clear enough for him to make out every finger on its hands.

Carly must've been caught up in the miracle of it all because she still hadn't objected to his presence. And he was glad. This was the most amazing thing he'd ever seen.

"Do you want to know if it's a boy or a girl?" the doctor asked. "Some parents want to be surprised."

Not Ian. He wanted to know. It would make the baby even more real for them. Maybe that would help them reach some kind of compromise that would leave them both happy.

And if truth be told, he didn't care one way or the other if they were having a son or daughter. He just wanted a healthy baby.

"Yes," Carly said. "I'd like to know." And then she glanced at Ian, her expression solemn—more like a grimace, actually.

He offered her a smile as an olive branch, but she didn't return it. At least she wasn't going to lay into him in front of the doctor and insist that he leave.

"In that case," the doctor said, "it's a girl."

At the revelation, a smile finally stretched across Carly's face. "Are you sure?"

The doctor chuckled. "Yes, I am. Congratulations." Then she paused the machine and introduced herself to Ian.

"It's nice to meet you," he said. "I didn't mean to interrupt."

"No problem. I'm glad you were able to join Carly." Then she went back to work, continuing the scan.

"That's amazing," Ian said as he continued to study the screen. "Look at that, Carly. She's sucking her thumb."

Carly swiped at the tears that had pooled in her eyes. "I can't believe that. We're having a little girl."

We. Ian was glad that she'd included him. And for a few magical moments, their conflict disappeared, and the wonder of new life took center stage.

He hoped the amazing feeling would last, but he suspected it was bound to end as soon as the exam was over.

Dr. Connor shut down the ultrasound, then reached for Carly's hand and helped her sit up. "I'll see you in three weeks."

Carly thanked her and stepped down from the table. As the doctor wheeled the machine out of the room, leaving her alone with Ian, she could finally let loose on him without embarrassing herself in front of her physician.

"What are you doing here?" she asked, her tone sharp.

"I came to see you. We need to talk."

Carly adjusted her blouse and grabbed her purse from the chair. "We definitely have a lot to discuss, but it could have waited until I got home."

"No, it couldn't. Besides, I'm glad I'm here. Seeing

our daughter on that screen was amazing. We're going to have a little girl, Carly. Can you believe it?"

She was thrilled, of course, but her anger at Ian and her sense of betrayal hadn't eased, and she wasn't sure it ever would.

How in the world could they ever be lovers again, or even coparent their daughter, if Carly couldn't trust him to be honest with her?

"We have some issues that might be insurmountable," she said.

He opened the exam room door for her. "I understand that, but give me a chance to explain myself."

Carly paused in the hallway. As she studied his remorseful expression, she was overwhelmed with emotion. She loved this man in spite of her anger and frustration. But she could only see heartbreak in their future.

As much as she'd like to tell him to take a permanent hike, he was right. They needed to talk, and it had been put off way too long.

"Okay," she said. "Let's find a quiet place where we can have some privacy."

Ten minutes later, after Carly made her next appointment, they left the parking lot in Ian's truck and drove to the community park a few blocks off Main Street.

As Ian pulled into a shady parking space, he asked, "Does this spot work for you?"

Carly scanned the stretch of grass, where a man threw a Frisbee to his golden retriever. Across the way, two young women sat on a bench near the playground, where several preschoolers climbed on a big, colorful jungle gym that had been set up in the sand.

"Sure," she said. "This is a good place to talk."

They exited his truck and made their way to a bench that was located away from everyone else.

"First of all," Ian said, "I was wrong for not being up-front with you, and I apologize. It won't ever happen again."

She wanted to believe him, but she wasn't sure she could.

"Why don't I start off by telling you everything?" he added. "How I met Felicia, why I quit singing with her and why I was so determined to have a quiet, peaceful life as a rancher."

"I'd like to hear it."

"Ask me anything you want to know, and I won't hold anything back."

"Okay. I know that you taught yourself to play the guitar, but when did you start playing professionally?"

"When I was seventeen. I was living in Fort Worth with my dad at the time. Most teenagers my age got fake IDs so they could drink and smoke. But I got mine so I could perform in a seedy neighborhood bar. A musician passing through heard me play one night and asked me to try out with his group. Before long, I traveled with the band to Nashville, where I eventually earned a name for myself."

"As Mac McAllister?"

"Yeah. One of the guys started calling me Mac, and the nickname caught on."

"When did you meet Felicia?"

"One day, when she was just starting out, she heard me play and hired me to be her lead guitarist. She could really rock the house with her voice, but she's always realized that a part of her success and popularity was due to my music and the songs I wrote. Trouble was, I'd always been an introvert and didn't like being forced into the limelight."

A light summer breeze whipped a strand of hair across her face, and she swiped it away. "But you said you didn't mind being on stage."

"Performing wasn't the problem. But Felicia began to place more and more demands on the band, our manager and on the people who hired us to perform. She thrived on the attention and fame, and it didn't take long for it to go to her head."

Carly asked, "Were you lovers at the time?"

Ian glanced at the man playing with his dog. "Yes, and both our personal and professional relationships soon became strained."

"So you broke up with her, quit the band and decided to live in obscurity for the rest of your life?"

"Not exactly. I joined another band, and Felicia flipped out. She set about having my new group's contracts cancelled."

"That's pretty vindictive. I'm surprised she had that much clout."

"I agree. She isn't a nice person and she exploits her fame at times."

Carly turned to the handsome cowboy, watched him as he studied the children on the playground. "How did you ever get involved with a woman like her in the first place? I'm not talking about performing with her. But as lovers. The two of you don't seem very well suited."

"It turned out that we weren't. But at first, our fit was magical on the stage. A romance seemed like a natural next step, but it didn't last very long. I soon found out how self-centered she could be."

"Did you end things then?"

"I wanted to, but I'd just found out that she was pregnant. I couldn't just leave her then. But she chose to have an abortion because a child would sidetrack her booming career. She didn't give it a second thought. On the other hand, I was crushed by the choice she made. I'd always wanted a family, and she knew it. But she made a unilateral decision that took the opportunity to be a father away from me. That's when I finally saw the real woman behind the fancy clothes and makeup."

"So you broke up?"

"The bright lights and glamour had really faded by then. So had the romance, especially when Felicia moved on to someone else."

"I'm sorry."

"Don't be. I really wasn't all that bothered by the breakup. The fact that Felicia cared so little about the child we created told me how she felt about me. And I realized that I wanted more from a lover or a lifetime partner." Ian turned to face her, his knee brushing hers. "That's why I didn't like you pressuring me to perform with you. It brought back too many bad memories."

She suspected the pregnancy had brought back bad memories, too, although he'd seemed happy about it. Delighted, actually.

"I'm sorry, Ian. I didn't mean to push you."

"Maybe not, but you ignored my feelings. I'm not trying to throw you under the bus, Carly, but I was afraid to level with you. I figured you'd work even harder to convince me to let you have your way. So, in truth, I wasn't the only one who created problems in our relationship."

Carly wanted to object, to say she hadn't tried to force his hand, but she had. "I'm sorry, Ian. I'll try not to push you anymore. You once mentioned that you'd seen me work my parents, and even though I hadn't wanted to admit it, you were right. I knew my dad's first reaction was to throw money at a problem, so I would use that to my advantage. And my mother would get so caught up in her own life that she sometimes forgot I existed, until I did something to remind her."

"I have a question for you," he said. "You're a beautiful and talented woman. There's no doubt in my mind that you'll hit the top of the charts. But are you determined to have a musical career because you truly want it? Or is it a way to show your parents—or rather, your mom—that you're someone special and important?"

Carly wanted to deny it, but she was afraid Ian had seen right through her. "I do want to sing and perform. I love being on stage. But you're probably right, at least partially. I do have a desire to show people that I count."

"You count to me."

She smiled. "Thanks. But to be honest, after meeting Felicia in the flesh today, I can see why I should think long and hard about what I want out of life."

"I'm glad to hear it. Not that I think you should change your mind. But I do hope you'll give your decision a lot of thought."

She studied the children on the playground, watched one of the moms push her daughter in a swing and listened to the child's squeal of laughter.

The person who'd taken Carly to the park when she'd been a child had been either Granny or one of the au pairs who'd watched her when her dad had been working and her mom had been on tour.

No way did Carly want that kind of life for her daughter.

A man and a boy walked out onto the lawn, carrying two mitts and a baseball. Her father hadn't spent any time with her brothers, either.

Carly turned to Ian. "I wish I'd had a chance to know the man you used to be—before Felicia."

"I'm still the same man, Carly. I'm just more guarded after what she put me through. You may not have seen it, but like I told you before, Felicia can be pretty selfish and vindictive."

"I saw that in her today," Carly admitted. The woman had a much different demeanor than the country-girl-next-door image she projected on stage.

"Well, I didn't see through her right away. I think that's because I wanted her to be the sweet, effervescent woman she pretended to be. I was young and naive, so I was caught up in it all."

"The fame?" she asked.

"No, it was never that. I just loved music and musicians. And I only wanted to play the guitar."

"And she wanted more from you?"

"Let's just say we never wanted the same things. And like she admitted earlier, she isn't one to take no for an answer."

Carly placed her hand on Ian's thigh, felt his warmth and strength. "I'm glad you realized what you wanted out of life. And I'm sorry that I pushed you so hard. I didn't realize what you were avoiding or why."

Ian reached for her hand, and she let his fingers curl around hers. "I love you, Carly. And if your career means that much to you, I'll let someone else buy the Leaning R and I'll go on the road with you. I'll be Mr. Mom while you perform."

Tears filled her eyes, and a rush of emotion built to an ache in her chest. "I love you, too. And I can't believe that you'd sacrifice your dream and happiness for me. No one has ever offered me that much before."

"You're every bit a star to me, Carly. I'm looking forward to seeing our little girl—and I'm hoping she'll be just like you."

Carly wiped her eyes. Seeing their little one on the screen had made her so real, so special, that she wasn't sure what she wanted anymore. Maybe she did want to spend time rocking her baby on a porch swing, picking huckleberries and baking one of Granny's yummy pies or even teaching her daughter to ride a pony.

"How can we make it work for all of us?" she asked him.

"When a man and woman love each other, anything is possible. Maybe we can become a songwriting team and try out the music and lyrics in front of an audience at the Stagecoach Inn."

"Then maybe it will work, Ian." She kissed him long and hard. When they came up for air, she smiled and said, "We'd better not get carried away here. Let's go home."

He stood and reached for her hand, drawing her to her feet. As they started toward his truck, she said, "Oh, I forgot to tell you. Jason called with some big news."

"What's that?"

"You know those twins he's bringing home to the States? He finally found out why our father was so intent on finding them. They're Rayburns, too."

"No kidding?" Ian asked as he opened the passenger door for her.

"I'm still trying to take it all in myself, but Jason is convinced. And I have no reason to doubt him. Just think. I have two more half siblings."

Ian cupped her cheek, his eyes glistening. "When it comes to family, I say the more the merrier."

"Something tells me you just might be right." She tossed him a happy smile. "Let's go home. I'm eager to unpack some of Granny's things and put the house back to rights."

Back to rights. Ian liked the sound of that, especially coming from Carly. They hadn't come up with a firm plan for the future, but they loved each other and wanted the best for their daughter.

On the drive back to the ranch, they talked about her

visions for the nursery as well as the way he wanted to fix up the house once the sale was final.

They'd no more than arrived at the Leaning R when Carly turned to him. "I'm glad we've agreed to be completely honest with each other and to come clean with everything."

"So am I."

"That's good, because talking about creating a nursery and refurbishing the ranch house got me to thinking. I owe you another apology."

Ian shut off the ignition, but he didn't even consider getting out of the truck. "What are you sorry for?"

"For assuming that you might not be able to come up with the money to buy this place. Now I realize that your 'little nest egg' is probably sizable."

"So what's wrong with coming to that conclusion?" he asked. "I never gave you any reason to think I had the kind of money to pull off a purchase like that."

"I know. But I should have trusted you when you told me that the purchase wouldn't be a problem. And I'm sorry I didn't."

He reached across the seat and took her hand. He rubbed his thumb against her wrist, felt the soft throb of her pulse. "You don't need to apologize for that. But from now on, we're both going to have to be completely honest and trust each other about everything."

She gave his hand an affectionate squeeze. "You're right. Why don't I go inside and fix dinner for us."

"Sounds good."

"Maybe you should bring a change of clothes and

your shaving kit when you come to eat. I'm looking forward to spending the night with you."

He flashed her a smile and winked. "That sounds even better. But just to make my intentions clear, I plan to spend every night together for the rest of our lives."

Fifteen minutes later, Ian had taken a shower and packed an overnight bag. But before leaving his cabin, he called Todd's cell number to check on Jesse Ramirez.

Todd answered on the second ring.

"What did you find out at the hospital?" Ian asked without preamble.

"Jesse has a bruised and swollen hand, but no broken bones, torn ligaments or tendons. I'm on my way right now to drop him off at his house."

"That's great news. Tell Jesse to take the rest of the week off, or even longer if that injury is still bothering him. I want that hand to heal completely—and before that first football game. I plan to be there, cheering him and the other boys on when Brighton Valley beats Wexler."

Todd laughed. "You and me both. Have a good evening, boss."

"Thanks. I intend to."

After disconnecting the line, Ian grabbed his overnight bag and took a sack of dog food out of the pantry. Then he went to the door and called Cheyenne. "Come on, girl. We're all going to have to learn how our family life is going to work. Let's go spend the night with Carly."

Cheyenne gave a little yip and wagged her entire hind end as if she knew exactly what he'd told her.

Then she dashed out the door and across the yard to the ranch house. She was waiting at the back door by the time his strides caught up with her.

They entered through the mudroom and caught the spicy aroma of sizzling meat, onions and peppers.

"Dinner smells good." He was going to like coming home each night.

Carly, who stood at the stove, flashed him a pretty smile. Then she lowered the flame on the burner.

Ian set Cheyenne's dog food on the table, and when Carly turned to face him, he swept her into his arms and placed his lips on hers. The kiss deepened, and their hearts beat in sync.

He wasn't sure how long the kiss lasted—long enough to catch the scent of scorching meat and veggies. Carly was the first to break away, as she removed the skillet from the flame.

Then she laughed. "I'd better focus on dinner, or we won't have anything to eat tonight."

"Right now, I'm only hungry for you. So a peanut butter sandwich a little later wouldn't bother me a bit."

"I have no problem postponing dinner, but I think I can salvage the chicken fajitas. Just give me a minute to put them into another pan."

As she took a spatula and scooped their meal out of Granny's cast-iron skillet, Ian eased behind her and brushed a kiss on her neck. "What's your calendar look like over the next few weeks?"

"Other than my doctor's appointment in three weeks, it's clear. Why?"

"I'd like to take you to Sarasota next weekend. My

grandparents are celebrating their fiftieth wedding anniversary with a big party."

"Seriously?" she asked. "That's awesome. I'd really like to meet them. I've never known a couple who've stayed married that long."

"And happily, too." Ian watched as she carried the skillet to the sink. "You might have to change the date of your next doctor's appointment."

"Why?"

"Because two weeks after their anniversary, I'm taking the family on a Mediterranean cruise."

Carly turned to him, her eyes lighting up. "I'd love to go with you. Whenever my parents went on a cruise, I had to stay home."

"Well, now it's your turn. I'll make the arrangements in the morning." He slipped his hand into hers, then led her out of the kitchen. "And as for Sarasota… I was planning to leave on Friday, but why don't we make a quick trip to Las Vegas first?"

She gave his hand a little tug. "For a cowboy who never wanted to leave the ranch, you certainly have a travel bug. Or are you a closet gambler?"

"I've never seen the fun in throwing money away. But I'd like us to get married before going to Florida, and that's the quickest way I can think of."

"Is that a proposal?"

He laughed. "If you plan to say yes and throw your arms around me, it is."

She tossed him an impish grin. "And if I don't give you that kind of reaction?"

"Then maybe we should take things day by day. But

it would be in our best interest to arrive in Sarasota as a married couple, especially since we'll be announcing that we're expecting a baby."

"Oh, now I remember. You mentioned that your grandparents were conservative churchgoers. I take it that a pair of wedding rings will put their minds at ease." She put her hands on her baby bump.

"That's not why I'm making the suggestion. They're not that stuffy. They'll accept you and our baby with open arms no matter what the circumstances."

"So the proposal has nothing to do with making me an honest woman?"

Ian pulled her into his arms. "Carly, you swept me off my boots the first day I laid eyes on you, and if I'd known how much I was going to love you, I would have proposed right then and there. But we had a few things to learn and get behind us first."

"You've got that right."

He smiled. "You know what? I once thought you had it all because of your parents and the Rayburn wealth. But I've realized that isn't true. You never had a real family."

"I have one now," she said.

"That you do." He brushed his lips across hers. "And I don't want to wait another day to make you my wife."

Carly raised up on tiptoe and slipped her arms around his neck. "Neither do I. Besides, I don't want our daughter to think we only got married because of her."

Ian chuckled.

"What's so funny?"

"I just thought of another good reason to tie the knot before we go. It'll make our sleeping arrangements better in Sarasota," Ian said.

"What do you mean?"

"My grandma is as sweet and gracious as can be, and you're going to hit it off immediately. But she's old-fashioned. She'll insist upon separate bedrooms if we're not married."

"She reminds me of Granny. I can't wait to meet her and your grandfather."

"I can't wait to introduce you."

As Ian led Carly to the bedroom, she asked, "You know what I think?"

"What's that?"

"The best limelights are those lit in the hearth at home."

A smile stretched across his face. "I couldn't agree more."

Then he proceeded to show her just how much he loved her, lighting a permanent flame in their hearts and souls.

Epilogue

Carly had been nervous about meeting Ian's family from the moment she boarded the flight in Houston, but she had no reason to be. Sean and Dottie McAllister were the sweetest and kindest couple she'd ever met.

The two had picked her and Ian up at the airport in Sarasota, then they'd driven them to their comfortable two-bedroom apartment in a seniors' complex not far from the home of their son and daughter-in-law, Roy and Helen.

Sean McAllister was a tall, slender man with silver hair, a twinkle in his blue eyes and an easy smile. He had a dry wit, which Carly could appreciate, and she warmed to him immediately.

The same went for Dottie. Ian's grandma wore her gray hair in an elegant French twist, but she was as down-to-earth as could be. She wasn't much taller than Carly, but she had a strong presence—and a loving heart.

The moment Ian introduced his new wife to his family, Dottie welcomed Carly into the fold with open arms. And news of the baby tickled her no end.

The woman who'd raised Ian truly was a lot like Granny, and Carly suspected the two would have become fast friends if they'd ever had the opportunity to meet.

The only down side was when Dottie mentioned her disappointment at not being invited to Carly and Ian's wedding.

"I hope you took plenty of pictures," she said.

Just one, actually. And Carly didn't have the heart to tell her that they'd said their vows at a chapel in Las Vegas with two strangers standing up with them as their witnesses.

"I'll tell you what," Ian said, "Carly and I will renew our vows after the baby is born, and you'll be at the top of our invitation list."

"Oh, good," Dottie said. "I'll make the cake."

For the first time in her life, Carly finally felt a part of something bigger than herself. And she was determined to provide that sense of love, acceptance and belonging for her child.

In fact, she intended to make sure that her brothers found the same thing, too. Jason appeared to have found it now that he had Juliana, but Braden deserved someone special, too.

Fortunately, the brothers' relationship had improved

considerably with their solving of the Camilla mystery. And they'd become closer than they'd been before, although Carly hoped they'd grow closer still, especially since they'd all have to figure out how to create a home and family for the twins. But that was something she'd deal with when she went home. In the meantime, she was enjoying every moment with Ian's family.

The anniversary celebration was held on Saturday afternoon in the rec room at the seniors' complex. Aunt Helen and Uncle Roy, who'd hoped to spring a surprise on the older couple, had decorated the room with balloons and various floral bouquets. But the secret was blown when one of the neighbors spilled the beans, telling Dottie and Sean she'd see them at their party on Saturday.

Nevertheless, the older couple was thrilled to know their new friends and neighbors had come together to share the day with them.

While the celebration was in full swing, Ian reached for his guitar, then took Carly's hand and led her to the front of the room, where a microphone awaited them.

"Are you ready?" he asked.

She smiled and nodded.

"While we're singing," Ian told her, "I want you to remember that, while I wrote the lyrics for them, every single word rings true for you and me. In fifty years, I want us to sing this at our own golden wedding anniversary."

Her heart soared with love for her new husband and the promise of a life together.

Ian stepped in front of the microphone. "On behalf of Sean and Dottie and their family, my wife and I would like to thank you all for coming out today to help them celebrate their anniversary. I've had the pleasure of knowing and loving this special couple all my life. And they were instrumental in making me the man I've become."

As the guests took their seats, Ian continued, turning to the celebrating couple. "Granddad and Grandma, I wrote this song just for you. And now my beautiful bride and I will sing it—as our gift to you."

As Ian began to strum the chords, Carly sang from the heart about a love that would last for all time. When they finished, everyone in attendance cheered and clapped in delight.

Ian slipped an arm around Carly and drew her close. "See, honey, I told you there would be plenty of opportunities for us to perform."

"I know. And I want you to know that I'm okay with being a local celebrity. As long as I can be a wife and mother, that's good enough for me."

He brushed a kiss on her lips. "You won't have to ever settle. Todd is proving to be a good ranch hand. I'm going to make him a foreman. Once the ranch is going strong again, I'd like to cut a record with you and even go on tour."

His offer surprised her—in part because it had come from his heart. She hadn't had to prod him, which was something she'd vowed not to do anymore.

"I'd love that, Ian. And I love you, too. You're the best thing that's ever happened to me."

"I'm the lucky one, honey."

She was glad he felt that way, but she still couldn't help thinking she was the one who'd gotten the better deal. If there's one thing Ian and his family had taught her, it was that the best gift in life was the heart of a cowboy.

* * * * *

Don't miss Braden Rayburn's story
in the next installment of
BRIGHTON VALLEY COWBOYS,
the new miniseries by
USA TODAY *bestselling author Judy Duarte.*
Coming soon to Harlequin Special Edition!

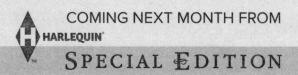

COMING NEXT MONTH FROM

HARLEQUIN®

SPECIAL EDITION

Available January 19, 2016

#2455 FORTUNE'S PERFECT VALENTINE
The Fortunes of Texas: All Fortune's Children • by Stella Bagwell
Computer programmer Vivian Blair believes the secret to a successful marriage is compatibility, while her boss, Wes Robinson, thinks passion's the only ingredient in a romance. When she develops a matchmaking app and challenges him to use it, which one will prove the other right...and find true love?

#2456 DR. FORGET-ME-NOT
Matchmaking Mamas • by Marie Ferrarella
When Dr. Mitchell Stewart begins volunteering at a shelter alongside teacher Melanie McAdams, he falls head-over-stethoscope for the blonde beauty. Once burned in love, Melanie's not looking for forever, even in the capable arms of a man like Mitchell. Can the medic's bedside manner convince Melanie to open her heart to a happy ending?

#2457 A SOLDIER'S PROMISE
Wed in the West • by Karen Templeton
Former soldier Levi Talbot returns to Whispering Pines, New Mexico, to make good on his promise to look after his best friend's family. The last thing he expects is to fall in love with his pal's widow, Valerie Lopez. Now, Levi's in for the battle of his life—one he's determined to win.

#2458 THE DOCTOR'S VALENTINE DARE
Rx for Love • by Cindy Kirk
Dr. Noah Anson's can-do attitude has always met with success, both professionally and personally. But when he runs up against the most stubborn woman in Jackson Hole, Josie Campbell, nothing goes the way he planned. It will take a whole lotta lovin' to win Josie's heart...and that's what he's determined to do!

#2459 WAKING UP WED
Sugar Falls, Idaho • by Christy Jeffries
When old friends Kylie Chatterson and Drew Gregson wake up in Las Vegas with matching wedding bands, all they want to say is "I don't!" But when they're forced to live together and care for Drew's twin nephews, they realize married life might be the happy ending they'd both always dreamed of.

#2460 A VALENTINE FOR THE VETERINARIAN
Paradise Animal Clinic • by Katie Meyer
Single mom and veterinarian Cassie Marshall swore off men for good when her ex walked out on her. But Alex Santiago, new to Paradise and its police department, and his adorable K9 partner melt Cassie's heart. This Valentine's Day, can the doc and the deputy create a forever family?

YOU CAN FIND MORE INFORMATION ON UPCOMING HARLEQUIN® TITLES, FREE EXCERPTS AND MORE AT WWW.HARLEQUIN.COM.

HSECNM0116

REQUEST YOUR FREE BOOKS!

2 FREE NOVELS PLUS 2 FREE GIFTS!

⊞ HARLEQUIN®

SPECIAL EDITION

Life, Love & Family

YES! Please send me 2 FREE Harlequin® Special Edition novels and my 2 FREE gifts (gifts are worth about $10). After receiving them, if I don't wish to receive any more books, I can return the shipping statement marked "cancel." If I don't cancel, I will receive 6 brand-new novels every month and be billed just $4.74 per book in the U.S. or $5.49 per book in Canada. That's a savings of at least 12% off the cover price! It's quite a bargain! Shipping and handling is just 50¢ per book in the U.S. and 75¢ per book in Canada.* I understand that accepting the 2 free books and gifts places me under no obligation to buy anything. I can always return a shipment and cancel at any time. Even if I never buy another book, the two free books and gifts are mine to keep forever.

235/335 HDN GH3Z

Name _____ (PLEASE PRINT) _____

Address _____ Apt. # _____

City _____ State/Prov. _____ Zip/Postal Code _____

Signature (if under 18, a parent or guardian must sign) _____

Mail to the **Reader Service:**
IN U.S.A.: P.O. Box 1867, Buffalo, NY 14240-1867
IN CANADA: P.O. Box 609, Fort Erie, Ontario L2A 5X3

Want to try two free books from another line?
Call 1-800-873-8635 or visit www.ReaderService.com.

* Terms and prices subject to change without notice. Prices do not include applicable taxes. Sales tax applicable in N.Y. Canadian residents will be charged applicable taxes. Offer not valid in Quebec. This offer is limited to one order per household. Not valid for current subscribers to Harlequin Special Edition books. All orders subject to credit approval. Credit or debit balances in a customer's account(s) may be offset by any other outstanding balance owed by or to the customer. Please allow 4 to 6 weeks for delivery. Offer available while quantities last.

Your Privacy—The Reader Service is committed to protecting your privacy. Our Privacy Policy is available online at www.ReaderService.com or upon request from the Reader Service.

We make a portion of our mailing list available to reputable third parties that offer products we believe may interest you. If you prefer that we not exchange your name with third parties, or if you wish to clarify or modify your communication preferences, please visit us at www.ReaderService.com/consumerchoice or write to us at Reader Service Preference Service, P.O. Box 9062, Buffalo, NY 14240-9062. Include your complete name and address.

HSE15

Closing her eyes for a moment, Melanie sighed. She had
no answer for the taunting voice in her head. No theory
to put forth to satisfy her conscience and this sudden,
unannounced huge wave of guilt that had just washed
over her like a tsunami after a 9.9 earthquake. And, like
it or not, that was what Mitch's kiss had felt like to her,
an earthquake. A great, big, giant earthquake and she
wasn't even sure if the ground beneath her feet hadn't
disappeared altogether, thanks to liquefaction. She felt
just that unsteady.

She'd stayed sitting down even after Mitch had left
the room.

*Damn it, the man kissed you. He didn't perform a
lobotomy on you with his tongue. Get a grip and get back
to work. Life goes on, remember?*

That was just the problem. Life went on. The love
of her life had been taken away ten months ago and for
some reason, life still went on.

Squaring her shoulders, she slid off the makeshift exam table, otherwise known in her mind as the scene of the crime, tested the steadiness of her legs and, once that was established, left the room.

Whether Melanie liked it or not, there was still a lot of work to do, and it wasn't going to get done by itself.

She had almost managed to talk herself into a neutral, rational place as she made her way past the dining hall, which, when Mitch was here, still served as his unofficial waiting room. That was when she heard Mitch call out to her.

"Melanie, I need you."

Everything inside her completely froze.

It was the same outside. It was as if her legs, after working fine all these years, had suddenly forgotten how to move and take her from point A to point B.

She had to have heard him wrong.

The Dr. Mitchell Stewart she had come to know these past few weeks would have never uttered those words to anyone, least of all to her.

And would the Mitchell Stewart you think you know so well have singed off your lips like that?

Don't miss
DR. FORGET-ME-NOT
by USA TODAY *bestselling author Marie Ferrarella,*
available February 2016 wherever
Harlequin® Special Edition books and ebooks are sold.

www.Harlequin.com

Love the Harlequin book you just read?

Your opinion matters.

Review this book on your favorite book site, review site, blog or your own social media properties and share your opinion with other readers!

Be sure to connect with us at:
Harlequin.com/Newsletters
Facebook.com/HarlequinBooks
Twitter.com/HarlequinBooks

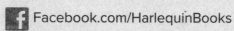
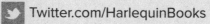